DEVIL

Archie Roy was one of Scc
time professor at Glasgow U
including six novels. A worl
ments of heavenly bodies, R(......iled to NASA
seeking his help in calculating .rajectories for space probes in the series of
lunar missions that led to the moon landing in 1969. But Roy was also an
investigator of the paranormal, bringing a scientifically rigorous approach
to the study of mediums and haunted houses and earning himself the nick-
name of 'Glasgow's ghost buster' in the process. His six novels, of which
Devil in the Darkness (1978) was the last, often blend elements of horror, science fiction, and thriller, and were well reviewed when originally published,
earning comparisons to H.G. Wells and John Buchan. Roy died at age 88 in
2012.

Greg Gbur is a professor of physics and optical science at the University
of North Carolina at Charlotte. He writes the long-running blog 'Skulls in
the Stars', which discusses classic horror fiction, physics, and the history of
science, as well as the curious intersections between the three topics. His
science writing has been featured in 'The Best Science Writing Online 2012,'
published by Scientific American, and his horror writing has appeared in a
number of volumes of the literary horror magazine *Dead Reckonings*. He has
previously introduced several John Blackburn novels for Valancourt Books.

Novels by Archie Roy

Deadlight (1968)
The Curtained Sleep (1969)
All Evil Shed Away (1970)
Sable Night (1973)
The Dark Host (1976)
Devil in the Darkness (1978)

Archie Roy

DEVIL IN THE DARKNESS

WITH A NEW INTRODUCTION BY
GREG GBUR

VALANCOURT BOOKS

INTRODUCTION

One of the challenges in writing a haunted house story – or, more generally, an 'Old Dark House' story whose horror may or may not be supernatural – is getting the characters into the house in the first place, and then keeping them there. Who would plausibly be willing to stay in a house where their lives or their very souls are endangered?

Looking at such fiction written over the years, three options are used quite commonly. The first of these is simply to have people take up residence in a house, not knowing that it has a supernatural threat inside. Novels such as 1977's *The Amityville Horror* (originally billed as 'a true story') and Michael McDowell's 1981 novel *The Elementals,* and movies such as 1982's *Poltergeist* take this approach. Often the unhappy homeowners are even stuck in the house once they learn its nature, either by financial necessity or, in the case of *Poltergeist*, by having one of their family members taken. In this framing, the reader is usually kept in the dark as much as the residents of the house, allowing the terror to build slowly through the story.

The second option for getting people into a haunted house and keeping them there it to force them to, usually via weather. The obvious example here is *The Shining* (1977) by Stephen King, in which the Torrance family is snowed in at the Overlook Hotel for the winter as dark forces inexorably drive Jack Torrance violently insane. Another example is the original 'Old Dark House' story, J. B. Priestley's 1927 novel *Benighted*, where Philip and Margaret Waverton are driven into a spooky mansion by a furious storm and flood. Trapping people in the house adds a nice touch of claustrophobia to what is hopefully an already tense tale.

The third option for drawing people into a haunted house is to use scientific curiosity. Paranormal researchers are natural protagonists for a ghost story: the helplessness of rational scientists in the face of the supernatural can heighten the feeling of dread. Furthermore, ghost hunters are rarely willing to leave

until a haunting has reached a truly catastrophic level. The group
that braves the unknown in Shirley Jackson's *The Haunting of Hill
House* (1959) learns this lesson too late, as the house claims one of
their own. In Richard Matheson's *Hell House* (1971), a physicist, his
wife, and two mediums are hired to investigate the titular house,
which corrupts them all with its malevolence.

In *Devil in the Darkness* (1978), Archie Roy ingeniously uses
all three methods at once. Paul and Carol Wilson, en route to
their honeymoon home in the Scottish Highlands, are sent off
course by an unseasonable blizzard. They seek shelter at the only
house they can find in the area: a sprawling and decrepit mansion,
which has just been occupied by a curious and eclectic group. We
eventually learn that the house is to be destroyed, and the new
residents are a combination of demolitions experts, on hand to
determine the best way to level the structure, and paranormal
researchers, present to hunt for signs of the supernatural before
the house is gone. Even when everyone learns of the danger in
the mansion, the storm forces them to stay and face it. A haunting that begins with simple bumps in the night escalates until it
become clear that none of the lodgers may survive their stay.

Scottish-born Professor Archie Roy (1924-2012) was uniquely
qualified to write a story about scientific investigations of the
paranormal. He was a stunningly accomplished astronomer,
earning his Ph.D. at the University of Glasgow in 1954 and joining
the faculty there in 1958. He was a prolific scientist, with over 70
scientific papers and multiple books on astronomical problems,
including *The Foundations of Astrodynamics* (1965) and *Orbital
Motion* (1978). As these titles indicate, he was a master of the
motion of objects through the cosmos, both spacecraft and satel-
lites (astrodynamics) and stars and planets (celestial mechanics).
His understanding of orbital motion led NASA to seek his help
calculating the trajectories of space probes in the 1960s; this work
culminated in the 1969 moon landing of Apollo 11. In recognition
of his achievements, Roy was made a Fellow of the Royal Society
of Edinburgh, the Royal Astronomical Society, and the British
Interplanetary Society. He also had an asteroid named after him:
(5806) Archie Roy, discovered in 1986.

Professor Roy also had another scientific passion, however: he was an active researcher in the paranormal, and is now remembered as much for his supernatural investigations as for his astronomical ones. His interest was sparked out of a chance encounter in the 1950s: one day, he became lost in the old university library and came across a section of books on spiritualism and psychic research. In Roy's own words (as reported in his obituary in *The Guardian* in 2013):

'My first ignorant reaction was "What is this rubbish doing in a university library?" But curiosity made me open some of the books. I was surprised to recognise some of the authors of this "rubbish", such as Sir Oliver Lodge, Professor William James, Professor Sir William Crookes, and so on. My balloon of ignorance was punctured by the needle of my scientific curiosity, and I found myself called up to a new career.'

Professor Roy pursued this new career alongside his scientific one for the rest of his life. He actively investigated hauntings, often at the request of home occupants who wanted to be rid of their supernatural tenants. He became a member of the London Society for Psychical Research, and 1987 he became the founding president of the Scottish Society for Psychical Research. He wrote a number of books on his paranormal work and the history of such research, including *A Sense of Something Strange, Investigations Into the Paranormal* (1990), *Archives of the Mind* (1996) and *The Eager Dead* (2008). Later in life, he became charmingly known as 'the Glasgow ghostbuster.'

It might seem somewhat surprising today to see a very distinguished physical scientist involved with the paranormal; however, as Roy himself noted above, there is a long history of talented physicists investigating the supernatural. British physicist Oliver Lodge (1851-1940), for instance, was one of the early researchers of electromagnetic radiation and consequently one of the pioneers of radio communication, but also was president of the London Society for Psychical Research at one time and a member of a group known as 'The Ghost Club.' Lodge thought that the existence of invisible electromagnetic radiation could provide a mechanism by which spirits could exist undetected alongside the living. Another example of a physical scientist with interest in the supernatural is English chemist William Crookes (1832-1919), who was a pioneer in the creation of vacuum tubes, and who studied X-rays and radioactivity during his career. Many people are familiar with his name due to his invention of the Crookes radiometer, a glass bulb containing windmill-like vanes inside that turn on their own when exposed to light. Crookes was also, however, active in The Ghost Club and the London Society for Psychical Research, and performed experimental tests of the abilities of many supposed mediums.

One significant difference distinguishing Lodge and Crookes from Roy, however, is the level of rigor of their spiritual studies. Even in their own time, Lodge and Crookes were criticized as being overly credulous of psychic claims and blasted as having run shoddy experiments of such claims. Professor Roy, however, was always skeptical and ran very rigorous tests that were often reported in the Scottish media. Perhaps reassured by this rigor, it is said that Roy's scientific colleagues enjoyed hearing his stories of haunted houses and mediums.

Roy's serious and calculated approach to testing psychic phenomena is very evident, even delightful to see, in *Devil in the Darkness*. The researchers in the book are very meticulous, exploring every possible non-supernatural explanation in detail before even considering a possible spirit. For example: when it is suspected that an additional unknown person might be in the house with them, the stranded group devises a plan to search the house, from bottom to top, sealing off and isolating every cleared section as they go. In many inferior horror stories, authors require their characters to do dumb things in order for the terror to proceed; in Roy's *Devil in the Darkness*, the characters are almost always making smart decisions, and horrible things happen in spite of their carefulness.

Looking at the dates of haunted house novels given at the beginning of this preface, one notes that many of them appeared in the 1970s, before Roy's *Devil in the Darkness*. One can't help but wonder if Roy read some of these contemporary works, particularly ones with paranormal researchers, and thought to himself in exasperation, 'I can write something better than these.'

Professor Roy was well-prepared to do so, not only due to his scientific and paranormal experience but also because of his skill as a writer. *Devil in the Darkness* was his sixth (and, it turns out, final) novel; his first, *Deadlight* (1968), appeared a decade earlier. His first three books have been characterized as science-based thrillers; the latter three are considered horror. Roy uses his formidable scientific knowledge to develop intriguing and unpredictable plots.

We have mentioned that haunted house novels typically use one of a few standard strategies to get the story going. It is also true that such novels usually end in one of a couple standard ways. One conclusion may be characterized as utter defeat: the residents of the house end up fleeing for their lives, none the wiser of the nature of the haunting. *The Amityville Horror*, *The Shining*, and *The Haunting of Hill House* all have this sort of ending. The other conclusion is revelation: the secret of the haunting is uncovered, possibly dispelling it in the process. *Hell House* and *Poltergeist* are examples of this form. Other stories may combine both types of ending. Without saying too much, it should be said that the house in *Devil in the Darkness* does have a terrible secret hidden within it that will be uncovered; it is a satisfying revelation that clearly draws upon Roy's own investigations and theories about hauntings.

So what we have in Archie Roy's *Devil in the Darkness* is a truly unique novel: a haunted house tale written by a man who was simultaneously a professional physical scientist, a professional author, and a professional paranormal investigator. His skills at all three endeavors shine through in the darkness of the story, which is well-crafted, creepy, and in the end genuinely satisfying.

So what did Archie Roy himself believe about the paranormal, in particular life after death? Like any good scientist, he refused to fully commit to a belief one way or another without compelling evidence. At one point, though, he gave a slight hint of his view, and his cleverness, saying, 'if I die and I find out I have not survived, I will be very surprised.'

Greg Gbur
September 2016

Where are the dead – those who have loved
us and whom we have loved; and those to whom
we have done some irreparable injury? Are
they gone from us for ever, or do they return?
Lord Halifax's Ghost Book

'I was not, and was content. I lived and did a
little work. I am not and believe not.'
Epitaph on the tombstone of
William Kingdon Clifford

Author's Note

It is perhaps needless to say that all the characters and incidents portrayed in this novel are fictitious. Nevertheless the books by Dr Ian Stevenson, Jeffrey Iverson and Dr Karl Wickland which are mentioned in the text are real and may be read by anyone interested in such matters. They will be found to be, at the very least, thought-provoking.

A.E.R.

Glasgow, 1978

1   White Wedding

The windscreen wipers were still able to cope, refusing occupation to the heavy cotton-wool flakes invading the screen in ever-increasing numbers. Inside the car it was warm. The metronome flick-flick of the wipers and the strain of peering through the swirling snowstorm added to his sense of dissociation. He blinked, feeling his eyes hot. Beside him the girl – his wife – peered at the one-inch-to-the-mile map.

'We turn left immediately we cross the stream.'

Her voice was soft, unworried as yet.

Outside the car daylight was fast yielding to dusk.

'Perhaps we should have stayed the night in Fort William,' she said. 'The forecast was bad.'

He opened his eyes wider, glanced at her.

'You found time on your wedding-day to watch TV?'

'Not me. Sister Jane. She said at breakfast that snow was threatened. "How on earth," she said, "will you while away the time if you're both snowbound in the cottage?"' She looked across at him, eyes wide and solemn.

'We may well find out,' he muttered, correcting an incipient skid. The car crossed the bridge and they were on a straight stretch. But the snow drove more fiercely at them now, borne on the wind funnelled by the unseen valley sides.

'We could turn back now,' he suggested. 'There was that village ten miles back.'

She shook her head.

'No, let's go on. It's barely fifteen miles now to the cottage. And everything's waiting for us. Dad had it fully provisioned and fuelled.' She leant across, touched his arm. 'Let's go on, Paul. I'd hate to begin my honeymoon in some bed-and-breakfast place.'

The little knot of anxiety tightened within him. Through the car's steering he could feel the road surface deteriorate minute by minute. And with the verges blotted out by the heavy snowfall he also knew he'd probably put the car into a ditch if he did try to turn.

'Wasn't there a junction we'd to look out for?' he remembered.

'Two . . . I think?' The map crackled. 'Yes. Three miles on.'

Scenes from the day's events flashed before him. His best man's joking. The church. The rows of 'friends and relatives' of the bride and groom. The wedding march – the deliberate turn of his head to see Carol, veiled and in white, escorted up the aisle by her father. His mouth twitched. How often in the early days of their engagement she'd sworn they'd never get her into that ridiculously primitive and outmoded outfit – anyway, it'd be a register office for her; she might go so far as to exchange jeans and shirt for a suit for the occasion. He let his foot ease up on the accelerator. God! It really was bleak outside.

The reception afterwards wasn't too bad. He couldn't really say he'd enjoyed the meal. The speeches were the expected mixed bag. Tim had gone a bit near the knuckle and he could have censored some of the telegrams, but everyone, even the maiden aunts, had taken it in good part. The dancing; the circulation among the guests – what an army of relatives Carol had – he'd have to get her to draw up some kind of family tree for him. He found himself grinning. She can do that at the cottage if we're snowbound and have, as sister Jane said, nothing better to do. A core of warmth formed within him and he thought: Of course she's right for us to press on.

Slipping away from the reception to change. The send-off. Not too riotous. The strange mixture of excitement and relief by the time they had driven out of Edinburgh on to the M9 for Stirling. They'd taken it in turns to drive, had something to eat at the Fort William Mercury Motor Inn. It had been raining hard even before they crossed the Rannoch Moor. And the snow had begun as they entered the outskirts of Fort William. It was utterly ridiculous. A blizzard in April.

The windscreen wipers were beginning to fail. By now inches of snow were caked on the screen in spite of the heater's blast of hot air; the clear wedge-shaped area was smudgy, like territory succumbing to defeat when a defence crumbles.

It was dark now. The girl had taken a torch from the glove

compartment to follow the map. The headlights' beams lit flurries of snowflakes or picked out the stark black branches of trees. The car descended a slope, engine whining in low gear. The road twisted and they were edging along an even narrower section, not much wider than the car, with a black drop on the right – to the sea? – and a streaming wet, near vertical wall of rock on the left. The car rattled across a wooden bridge.

He risked a glance at the dashboard. Surely they had come far enough? They seemed to have been journeying blindly for hours over the Ardnamurchan Peninsula. His sense of impending catastrophe strengthened when he read the mileometer. In the heady planning of this trip, Carol and he had pored over maps, measuring, estimating how far the cottage was from Edinburgh. And now the mileometer told him they had covered a distance in excess of seven miles farther than they should have from Fort William.

He drew up, slipped the gear lever into neutral.

'I think we're lost,' he said. He switched on the interior light. 'Let me see the map.'

Without a word she handed it across. He followed the road on the map, tracing its route from Lochailort along the coast before it curled round the flanks of Sgurr Dhomhuill Mor. He remembered crossing the river Moidart, a black spate-swollen flood, then coming down towards the little village of Kentra. All that he remembered. They had struck off due west at that point. But beyond that . . .

He rubbed his aching eyes. If they had been on the right road there should have been no climb up this cliff road. Where on earth could they be?

The wind howled and they felt the car cringe under its onslaught. The girl shivered in spite of the warmth.

'We can't turn here.'

'I know. We go on. But be prepared to spend your wedding night in the back of this car.'

'In a blizzard.' She summoned a smile. He smiled back.

'Don't worry. There may be a house or a village at the end of this road. It can't go on forever.'

He wondered if he sounded convincing.

He put the car in gear, let in the clutch. The wheels spun, squealing. He tried again, gingerly. The car moved forward. The road was dropping now, so fast he dare not change out of lowest gear. The car showed a tendency to weave. The easiest touch swung the steering wheel. Hunched forward, he peered ahead. The steep slope on the right melted back to be replaced by snow-laden trees; on the left the drop gave way to rising wooded ground. The blizzard was appalling now in its cold fury. Thoughts of people found frozen to death in cars came to him. He seemed to remember reading that leaving the engine running to heat the car produced death by carbon-monoxide poisoning. And if not – after the petrol ran out – what then?

Carol gripped his arm.

'I see a light!'

'Where?'

'To the left!'

He saw nothing in the swirling snow but black clumps of trees. He slowed the car.

'Do you still see it?'

'No. It's gone.'

'I'll go forward slowly. Was it ahead of us?'

'Yes.'

The beams of the headlights showed a bend in the road, towards the left. He drove to it, stopped and switched off the lights. And then he saw it too, faint, distant but unmistakable.

'There! Do you see it?'

'Yes. That's what I saw. It must be a house.'

'All right. Keep your eyes on it. I've got to concentrate on the road. Tell me if it disappears again.'

'I still have it, Paul. Go ahead.'

The car nosed forward. The ground was rising again, but not steeply. The narrow road turned again.

'I've lost it!' Her voice was brittle, more high-pitched than usual.

'It's all right. I think the trees are hiding it.'

Another bend negotiated and he heaved a sigh of relief as the light reappeared. Brighter now. The girl leaned forward.

'It must be a house – a big one.'

It dawned on him that they were approaching it along a drive-way between wooded grounds. The beams from the car's head-lights swung across an open area of unknown extent masked by myriads of tumbling driving snowflakes. Passing over a building of substantial size, they lit up vehicles standing in front of the house. Their heavy mantles of snow effectively disguised their outlines though one, far larger than the other, seemed to be some kind of van.

The main light came from a slit between curtains at a window. Paul drew up the car as near as possible to what seemed to be the main door, revealed by the car's lights. In their beams he had clearly made out broad steps between stone pillars. He put the car in neutral, but kept the engine running.

'At least there's someone at home,' Carol said. 'Could it be a hotel?'

'I don't know. At any rate we'll find out where we are.' He hesitated. 'Look, darling. If it is a hotel or even a boarding house and there's accommodation, shall we stay here the night?'

'Find out first.' In the faint greenish light from the dashboard he saw her frown. 'Find out, Paul.'

'All right. I won't be long.'

Opening the door he slid outside, closed it quickly and trudged through the snow, its icy bite sinking into his ankles. He gasped as the wind slashed a flurry of ice at his back. Once up the snow-covered steps under the stone lintel supported by the pillars he found it less open. He searched for a bell-push, pressed it and heard nothing. He tried to control his shaking frame and only made it worse. The wind howled and a branch from a tree crashed down. He thumped the door. Dammit! I know there's someone in. Are they stone deaf? Surely they wouldn't refuse to open the door on a night like this. . . .

Behind the leaded glass panels a light glowed and moved. It brightened. The door opened. A bearded man, his hand holding a large torch, stared at him. His face was a negative in the upflung light.

The man gestured with the torch, and stepped back.

'Come in, come in!'

He entered the house, entered a darkness enhanced rather

than dispersed by the solitary torchbeam. He felt spaciousness – large hall? – and a musty unused smell – dry-rot? – reached his nostrils.

'Follow me.'

The pool of light from the torch moved away to the right. A door opened and brighter light blazed through the widening gap. Voices came to his ears. His guide's body momentarily filled the gap, went through and he followed.

Paul's first impression was of a large room filled with people standing or sitting, either at a big, central dining-table or on the floor near a log fire burning brightly in a handsome fireplace. The room's illumination came from four oil-lamps. Some sort of meal was in progress – an alfresco one since dishes were scattered not only on the table but before the people sitting on the floor. Even those few people standing were eating from the plates they held. There must have been eight or nine men and women in the room. They wore a variety of clothes, from ski-outfits to lounge-suits; their ages seemed to range from early twenties to late fifties.

On his entry, conversations died and the room's occupants turned to face him, curiosity evident in their eyes.

He had stopped shivering but was miserably conscious of his wet, clammy trouser legs and socks.

'I'm sorry. My wife and I seem to be lost. We are making for Shona Cottage. Perhaps you can tell me how to get there?' What is this place? he wondered. A private house?

A man in his fifties, bespectacled, with a fleshy face and untidy grey-brown hair, rose from the table.

'Your wife? Where is she?'

'Outside in the car.'

'Outside! Hunt, do go and bring her in.'

The bearded man left the room. Paul found himself protesting.

'There's no need. If you could just give me directions . . .'

The older man gestured towards the fire.

'Come over and warm yourself.' He allowed himself to move towards the fireplace. The others still watched him. The bespectacled man hesitated.

'It's a bit awkward.' Someone laughed, a short bark of laughter; the speaker turned his head sharply, then looked at Paul again. 'Do you know these parts?'

'No, I'm afraid not. Nor does my wife – at least not well. Where are we?'

'This is Ardvreck House.'

His eyes scanned Paul's face, as if expecting some sort of reaction.

'You don't know it?'

'No. Is it far from Shona Cottage?'

The man sighed. 'My dear fellow, I haven't the faintest idea.' He turned to the others. 'Does anyone know?' No one answered. 'I'm afraid we're all strangers here too.'

Paul's bewilderment grew. All of them strangers? Who were they? Out of the corner of his eye he saw a man step forward. He was in his early thirties, with a lean, capable face and reddish hair cut unfashionably short back and sides.

'I've got a map in my things. I'll get it.'

He left the room. Within seconds the door opened again and the bearded man ushered in Carol. Her sheepskin coat was powdered with snow, her dark hair glistening wet. Her eyes swept the company, her face relaxed a little on seeing Paul. As she crossed to him, the door reopened and the red-haired man entered. He strode across to the table, cleared away cups and plates to provide an area on which to spread out the map. A dark man, in his forties, with a sardonically clever face, spoke for the first time.

'How is it outside?'

The bearded man brushed snow from his face.

'It's worse. A regular white-out. What the hell is the British weather coming to? Droughts, monsoons, blizzards.'

Paul squeezed Carol's arm encouragingly before going to the table. The red-haired man's forefinger stabbed at the map.

'Here we are. Where were you going?'

A wave of dismay swept over Paul as he orientated himself and saw the distance between Shona Cottage and Ardvreck House. How could they have gone so far wrong? Twelve miles as the crow flew – and few crows would be flying on a night like this. By road, or by the single tracks that passed for roads, nearer twenty.

He visualized the arctic-like conditions outside, remembered the way the car had slithered sickeningly on ice on the cliff-road. He indicated the cottage's position. For all he knew the four-mile track up to the cottage was impassable by now. And there seemed to be no sign of any house, let alone village or hotel, between here and the cottage.

The red-haired man straightened up.

'Not good,' he said. More to the company than to Paul he added: 'In fact I'd say you'd be downright foolhardy to try to make it tonight.'

His words echoed Paul's own thoughts. In his exhaustion he noted the dismay not only on Carol's face but on the bespectacled man's features. And with the prospect of spending the night here – surely they wouldn't refuse them shelter? – he looked at the room and company more closely than he had done before. And found his own dismay deepen to uneasy and wary speculation.

2   An Uneasy Haven

In spite of the cheerfully crackling log fire and its output of warmth, it was a drab, dingy dining-room, badly in need of redecoration. Old threadbare, dark brown curtains hid all five windows in the big bay window pushed out of one corner of the room. Missing hooks let them sag in places like a slattern's skirt. Two other windows, also curtained, pierced the walls adjoining the bay window. The fourth wall contained a panelled double door, flanked by a massive Victorian mahogany sideboard to the left and a glass-fronted display cabinet to the right. The wallpaper was embossed, carrying a turgidly uninspired pattern in browns and greens. Its faded quality was emphasized by the rectangular, brighter gaps on the walls where pictures had once been hung. In two of the dark ceiling corners the paper curled tiredly away from the walls.

The bespectacled man seemed worried; the dark sardonic man seemed content to be an amused spectator. The other members of the company listened interestedly. The bespectacled man pushed his glasses on to the bridge of his nose.

'Well, obviously you can't go on tonight.' He frowned. 'It's rather awkward, though.'

'Perhaps you'd better put them in the picture, Meredith,' the sardonic man suggested. Meredith flicked an angry glance at him before turning back to Paul.

'You must understand,' he said slowly, 'that we ourselves arrived here only three hours ago. When the blizzard struck we still hadn't unpacked half our stuff.' He hesitated. 'We've been trying to make ourselves comfortable. You see the house hasn't been lived in for fifteen years.'

Looks more like fifty, Paul thought. Who were these people? The new owners? As if in answer to his unspoken questions, Meredith said: 'Look, let me introduce ourselves. I'm Brian Meredith.' He indicated the sardonic man, the bearded man and the red-haired man in turn: 'Arnold Bourne and Jeremy Hunt. This is Captain Pollard. Over there Ann Parish, Harry Fletcher and Joyce Mair.' The last three comprised a brown-haired attractive woman in her mid-twenties, a plump, fair-haired, balding young man in a brown leather jerkin, a white, roll-necked sweater and denims, and a woman, about thirty, with jet-black hair. In various ways, by nod, or smile, or the raising of a hand they acknowledged the introduction. Paul smiled at them.

'I'm Paul Wilson. This is my wife Carol.' His eyes met hers and he knew with a small warm feeling of pleasure that she was mentally echoing his thought that this was the first occasion he had introduced her as his wife.

Meredith stepped forward.

'Well, we shall have to get a room ready for you.'

He crossed to a small occasional table by the bay window, clicked open a briefcase lying there beside the oil-lamp and drew out some papers. He consulted them.

'Only two bedrooms unoccupied – one and seven.' He squeezed his lower lip between thumb and forefinger. 'Better be one. It's bigger and anyway seven has that broken window.' He raised his head. 'We'd better have a look at seven again and try to put a board or something over that window. The snow must be getting in.'

Captain Pollard nodded.

'I'll see to that now.' With a quick smile at the Wilsons he strode out of the room.

The black-haired woman rose from her seat before the fire, uncurling with an almost feline grace.

'And I'll organize something to eat. You must be famished. We can run to hot soup, cold meat, veg and potatoes, some dessert. How will that do?'

Paul and Carol spoke together.

'Marvellous –'

'That'll be fine –'

At the closed double door the woman stopped.

'Harry, come and help me.'

The balding man rose, moved towards her. He grinned.

'Afraid of the –'

'Harry!' Meredith's voice interrupted him sharply. 'Perhaps you'd better see how Sergeant Smith and – uh – Mr Swanson are getting on. They'll need something to eat.'

Carol thought: What was Harry going to say? There are two more we haven't seen. 'Captain' and 'Sergeant'! What have we here? The army? Mr Meredith almost forgot the second one's name. I don't like the man Bourne. He's apart from everyone else, feels superior. Meredith was using a map of the house. What sort of situation is this when the owner – is he the owner? – has to use a map of his house? I wish we were at the cottage. I hate the idea of staying here tonight. She listened to the wind mourn its inability to penetrate the warm room.

Meredith said: 'Ann, let's check on the number of blankets airing in the sitting-room.'

And now Bourne and Hunt were alone with them in the room.

The sardonic man rested a hand on the mantelpiece, drew it away, grimaced at the smudges of dust on his fingers and brushed at them with the other hand.

'Have you travelled far today?'

'From Edinburgh.'

'Indeed. Quite a journey.'

Paul felt the newly-weds' reluctance to provide information.

'I'd better get our cases out of the boot. Can I borrow one of these torches?'

Jeremy Hunt stirred.

'Of course. Look, I'll come with you. Hold the torch and keep the car door open while you rummage around. Make it quicker. Okay?'

'Thanks.'

As the dining-room door closed, Carol, conscious of Bourne's eyes on her face, thought uneasily: Why does everyone have to move about in pairs in this place? Except the soldier.

The double doors opened and two men entered. The taller, with straggly shoulder-length brown hair, was about thirty years of age. He wore a thick grey pullover over dark-blue corduroy trousers tucked into black zip-up boots. The other, more chunky in build, was a few years older. He wore a red-and-black-check woollen shirt and fawn trousers. His grey hair, like Pollard's, was cut short back and sides. Both men were dirty and cobwebbed; both carried four oil-lamps each, unlit. They halted, eyed Carol speculatively.

'Where's everyone?' Even as he spoke, Carol saw the grey-haired man check her left hand.

'Doing various jobs,' Bourne replied. 'How did you get on?'

'No luck. That generator needs stripping and cleaning. Probably new wiring. It's as damp as the bottom of a duck pond down there.' He set down his burden of lamps. 'Damn' cold, too.'

The chunky man spoke in a cockney accent.

'Bit of luck, though. Found these. And two drums of paraffin.'

Bourne nodded.

'Well, you'd better get cleaned up. There's more food on the way. By the way. This is Mrs Wilson. She and her husband will be staying the night here. Refugees from the storm.' To Carol he added: 'Cliff Swanson and Sergeant Ted Smith.'

The dining-room door opened to readmit Paul and Hunt. Each carried a travelling case; each man's hair was wind-blown, with snow scattered thickly over their hair and clothes. They dropped the cases, brushed themselves down before the fire.

During the next hour Carol and Paul's dream-like state took greater and greater hold upon them. The hot food and drink, the jumbled highly emotional events of the day, the fierce cold and strain of the latter part of their journey, the disorientation and incomprehension they felt in this grubby house with its diverse group of occupants all conspired to dull their senses.

People came and went – usually in pairs, Carol noted almost obsessively; oil-lamps were taken to be filled and shared out; conversations were elliptic, short and difficult to grasp; dishes were cleared away. Meredith wrote industriously at the table in the bay-window area. Finally he got up and distributed sheets of paper to everyone, including the Wilsons. When they looked at these they found they held duplicated diagrams of the ground and first floors of the house. They saw that the bedrooms were numbered one to seven in Roman numerals, the bathrooms one to three. Even the furniture had been included and labelled. Underneath the first-floor plan there had been added in ink a list of names with bedroom numbers attached.

'Now,' said Meredith. 'This lack of electric light is very unfortunate but if we are systematic about things there should be no trouble. We have sufficient oil-lamps from the house and our own Tilley lamps to provide two lamps to each room, that is to bedrooms upstairs and lounge and dining-room downstairs. And each person can have one electric torch. Make sure each person has matches or a cigarette lighter. The three bathrooms are in working order, though I am afraid there is no hot water.'

How did they cook tonight? Carol wondered. Calor-gas stoves, I suppose.

Paul thought: Meredith talking like this reminds me of something. What is it? Why yes. He's like a general addressing his troops before they go over the top. And he suddenly realized that Meredith was speaking to him.

'Sorry, I'm afraid I was miles away.'

'I was saying that after your journey you two probably want an early night. We've put your room in order, as far as we are able to. You'll even find a couple of hot-water bottles in your bed. Courtesy of the house. So if you'd like to . . .'

It's almost as if he's sending us off like children to bed, Paul thought, so that the grown-ups can talk in adult fashion. His tiredness was such, however, that he felt no desire to linger let alone resent their dismissal. He picked up the cases. Ann Parish handed Carol two torches. She glanced at Meredith.

'We'll guide you to your room. In case you lose your way.'

The hall had one oil-lamp casting its mellow glow over the stairs, a bare floor and panelled walls. A passageway on either side of the stairs led away into blackness. Meredith, carrying a lamp, led the way to the first floor. Great pools of shadow fled from his patch of light to scurry behind it and re-form in the rear.

They climbed to a landing that ran round all four sides of the stairwell. Above the well a large domed cupola of many panes was black under its weight of snow.

The Wilsons' bedroom was a mirror-image of the dining-room downstairs. Its bay window was curtained. The bed was a huge double one, old-fashioned and massive, as was the tall, heavy walnut wardrobe to the right of the door and the two dressing-tables. Two oil-lamps, one on each dressing-table, were already lit.

Meredith and Ann Parish entered the room with them.

'I'm afraid it's pretty cold and uninspiring,' he apologized. 'But the bedclothes have been aired. As you'll see from the charts I've given you, the nearest bathroom is at this side of the house, two doors in the direction of the dining-room.' He watched Paul hoist a case on to the bed. 'There are no oil-lamps in the bathroom so you'll need to take your own illumination with you.'

For all his seeming desire to pack the Wilsons off to bed, Meredith showed a strange reluctance to leave them. Paul snapped open the case and froze. Scattered liberally over the clothes folded inside was a multicoloured snowstorm of confetti. Damn Tim, he thought. He must have doctored the case while we were changing. It was obvious from Meredith's face and that of Ann Parish that they had seen the evidence. Dismay and sympathy were their predominant reactions. Meredith sighed.

'My dear Mr and Mrs Wilson. What rotten luck to spend your wedding-night in a cold, chilly snowbound dump like this.' He raised both hands. 'Look. My advice, for what it's worth, is to get a good night's sleep, drive off in the morning to your cottage and forget you ever were here.' He turned to the woman. 'Come on, Ann. Let's wish our guests as good a night as possible in the circumstances and take ourselves off.'

When the door closed, Paul and Carol stood facing each other. The girl essayed a smile.

'I don't know whether to laugh or cry.'

He crossed to her and put his arms round her.

'Look, darling, I don't quite know how to put this. And for heaven's sake don't get me wrong. But perhaps we should take Meredith's advice.'

She looked up at him.

'What do you mean?'

'Well, I mean, we're tired – this room is like an icebox – the whole place is so dreadfully off-putting – perhaps we should just try to get some sleep and get away from here in the morning.' He glanced anxiously at her. 'I mean, I'm not – it's not as if I don't want – '

She smiled, her forefinger across his lips.

'I do love you, Paul. I know exactly what you mean. Let's consider our honeymoon to begin tomorrow.'

They unpacked only what was strictly necessary from their cases. Paul made a first reconnoitre from the room to the bathroom. When he returned he gave Carol directions and she left.

Never in my wildest dreams did I expect it to be like this, he thought later as they lay under the blankets, old-fashioned stone hot-water bottles at their feet, the one dimmed oil-lamp Carol had unashamedly insisted on casting a pale circle of illumination on the high, plastered ceiling. She lay in his arms, turned towards him, her eyes open. To undress on one's wedding-night in a sexless unheeding haste, to scramble into bed pursued not by desire but by the frigidity of the room, to lie in bed obsessed with uneasy speculations concerning the purpose of the occupants now presumably making ready for their own retiral to sleep was quite staggeringly improbable.

Gradually their chilled bodies thawed and warmth returned.

Carol murmured, her breath faint against his face: 'There's something very, very strange about these people.'

'Perhaps.'

'Do you realize they haven't told us anything about themselves, or where they come from?'

'Yes.'

He pulled her towards himself, kissed her. Her lips were warm and soft. Gently he inserted his cupped hand between her legs and held her for a long moment.

'Go to sleep,' he said. 'The sooner you're asleep the sooner it'll be morning.'

In response, she touched him.

'Why,' she said, softly and sleepily, 'I do believe someone will be fully recuperated by tomorrow.'

'That you can depend on,' he whispered.

She sighed happily and turned round so that her back fitted snugly against his front. Almost immediately his consciousness began to dissolve, hypnagogic imagery drifting before him until sleep came.

3   The Night Walker

He awoke suddenly, not in the gradual manner he was accustomed to, but instantly alert as if consciousness had reintegrated as quickly as a stretched rubber band snaps together when released. He was lying flat on his back, his body cocooned in warmth, his face cold in the icy air of the room. Moisture from his exhaled breath had dampened the blanket round his mouth.

Carol's warm back touched his left arm. He lay without moving, watching the ceiling. The faint light from the dimmed oil-lamp still rendered the room visible. He had no idea how long he had slept or what had wakened him. He stretched out his right hand to the top of the small bedside cabinet and retrieved his watch and a torch. Shielding the beam with the fingers of one hand, he contrived to read the time. Twenty past two.

And then he heard the noise. It came from the ceiling. The sound of footsteps. A heavy, measured tread back and forth, from the area of the bay window to the centre of the room. Back and forth. The sound of a heavy man's regular pacing. Paul could almost visualize him, hands clasped behind his back, striding in deep thought across the floor of the room above. The room above? Was there another floor to the house?

Who was it? And at nearly half past two. Which of the nine

people they had met was up there? But if he remembered correctly they were all allocated to bedrooms on this floor. Was it someone he and Carol had not yet met, someone hidden away from them? Half-formulated speculations he had not dared to voice to Carol surfaced in his mind again. That this group of people had no permission to be in this dilapidated house at all – that they had some illegal purpose – that the army-type men were bogus – that he and Carol were in some kind of deadly danger. Before, those thoughts had seemed melodramatic; now in the low-confidence hours of the night he was not so quick to dismiss them.

And now the sounds changed and it seemed as if a heavy box or trunk was being dragged across an uncarpeted floor. How Carol could sleep through the noise beat him. . . . But the slow regular rhythm of her breathing continued.

Gently he pulled back the bedclothes and slid out of bed. Almost immediately he began shivering as the chill air drained his body heat. Quickly he put on slippers and the new dressing-gown Carol had given him. He crossed to the bay window and drew the thick, musty curtain aside. Total blackness lay outside with no moon to light up the surrounding countryside. Not even a star. And if any room on the two sides of the house meeting at this corner was illuminated it must have its windows tightly curtained. A trunk rumbled across the ceiling again. What on earth were they up to?

He padded across to the dressing-table and picked up the diagrams of the house. In the pool of light from the torch he checked the bedroom allocation. He had remembered correctly. According to the list, they were all sleeping on this floor.

He was about to lay the sheets of paper down when he noticed the narrow flight of stairs ascending from the end of the corridor in which the door to their bedroom lay. So there was an upper storey, the plans of which had been kept from them. Why?

He glanced across at Carol, lying curled on her side under the bedclothes. He was seized with completely conflicting needs – to get out of this ice-house atmosphere back into bed beside her where warmth and sleep could be found, and to find out what was going on upstairs. The second desire appalled him. It seemed foolhardy and reckless in the extreme. He looked at the ceiling again. From the centre of an ornamental plaster rose dangled the electric light, in a big old-fashioned grubby shade. He saw that the disturbance upstairs had set it swaying gently to and fro at the end of its thick flex. As a fresh thump occurred, he saw it quiver. The bulb tinkled in its holder.

He was not aware of having made any decision. With an odd feeling of detachment he found himself opening the bedroom door and peering through the gap. The stairwell was pitch-black. Indeed it was impossible in the total blackness to make out any part of the first floor.

Now, he thought. Now is the time to close the door and go back to bed. If you go along that corridor to the left, Carol might wake up and find you gone. She'd be scared stiff. That's a good sensible reason for getting back to bed.

It'll only take a minute, part of him said. He switched on the torch and sent its beam along the corridor. It lit up the black, opaque panes of a window in the far wall at the end of the corridor. He moved it to the left and it revealed a dark rectangular opening and the first treads of an ascending flight of stairs.

Paul realized he was apprehensive, that the chill in his bones was as much due to fear as to the low temperature of the surrounding air. And then quite suddenly he capitulated to his self-respect. Quickly he approached the narrow stairway, the light from his torch slanting up a drab dark-green wall holding a wooden rail angled upwards.

Ten steps upwards the flight turned left. Grimly he went upwards, the beam searching before him.

At the top of the flight he halted. Directly in front of him, a long, low, narrow corridor ran away, parallel to the front of the house. The light from his torch seemed powerless to penetrate fully the deep palpable blackness filling the tunnel-like passage beyond. In any case, he knew it was the other corridor leading off to the right that must take him to the door of the room above their bedroom.

His stomach a knot of tension, he padded along the ten feet of corridor to the closed door on his right. No light came from under it. And no sound from behind it. Around the oval of his torch beam, the darkness pressed in with claustrophobic intensity, combining with the chill of the air to produce in him an impression of being shut in an ice house.

What do I want, what do I want? he found himself gabbling inwardly. If I open that door and they're behind it – doing what? – what happens then? But maybe it's locked. Maybe they've gone now, gone while I stood at the bedroom door. They could have departed along that other corridor.

He tried the handle. It turned, slowly, reluctantly. And the door gave inwards when he applied pressure to it. And a black, totally black gap appeared.

He pushed the door wider, sent the torch beam around the high ceilinged seven-sided room, five of whose sides held windows. Light splashed from dusty bare floorboards, several cupboards, a central octagonal table and four chairs. But nothing else. If boxes and trunks had been stored there, they had been taken away. Trembling with a sense of outrage at the way he had been put through an emotional wringer, Paul turned to go. And froze, as two facts about the room grabbed at him, shredding his anger-built ego.

There were no curtains, not even a curtain-rail. And though his footprint was plain in the layer of dust on the floorboards by the door, there were no other marks.

Down below, he had stood at the bedroom window looking outside while the sounds of footsteps and trunks being dragged across the floor above came to him. It had been pitch black outside, without the slightest illumination spilling outside from this room, this room with uncurtained windows.

Quite suddenly he felt vulnerable in the most dreadful way as if dissolution was imminent. Layers of ice formed within him; his teeth began to chatter. The torch beam shook. His mind became totally possessed with the transient nature of life and the certainty of the grave's final cold embrace. He was a man utterly lost, drained of every scrap of hope, afraid for his very soul's existence.

A vision of Carol lying downstairs flashed before his mind. The fear of the torch failing and leaving him in total darkness up here suddenly overwhelmed him. A tiny, isolated bit of him listened amazedly to someone whimper – himself – before he turned and fled the icy room, padded as fast as he could to the head of the narrow flight of stairs and descended, slippers slap-slapping on the bare treads, to hasten in mindless terror back to his bedroom.

Carol still slept. Panting like a dog, his heart thumping within his chest, he shut the door, crossed to the oil-lamp and turned it up to brighten the room. He threw off dressing-gown and slippers, slid into bed and lay down, taking care his trembling body did not touch Carol's. His feet, two blocks of ice, sought the comfort of the hot-water bottle, still warm. Great fits of shivering shook his frame. In the semi-darkness his eyes searched the ceiling. There was absolute quiet up there now.

What in God's name have we got into? he thought.

With no hope of achieving sleep, he tried to relax to control the endlessly cycling constructs of his overwrought imagination, to wait out the last long hours of the night. Gradually warmth came to him again and he fell into an exhausted, disturbed sleep just before the first grey light of dawn began to filter through the dirty panes of the window he had left uncurtained.

4   Journey in an Empty Landscape

The sound of knocking wakened him. Disorientated with lack of sleep, he lay trying to place the source of the noise. He felt his mind tinged with that vague sense of anxiety so often associated with the brain's return to consciousness after an unpleasant dream.

The knocking was repeated. Carol stirred beside him and he finally realized it came from the door.

'Mr and Mrs Wilson? Good morning! Breakfast downstairs in twenty minutes. Okay?'

Was it Meredith? The thick door so muffled the voice that he couldn't be sure.

'All right,' he called back. 'Thank you. We'll be down.'

Evidently they weren't going to let them have a long lie. Was this an indication of a desire to send them on their way as fast as was decently possible? Stretching out his hand, he found his watch and looked at it. He noted with surprise that it was nine-five. Not so early. He lay back, gazing at the dingy ceiling. The events of the night seemed unsubstantial. But he knew he had not dreamed them.

Carol propped herself up on an elbow and looked down at him.

'Good morning,' she said. 'Now just give me time and I'll remember the name. Is it George? No. It's Tom.' She contrived intense, frowning concentration. 'Why no! It's Paul. Hello, Paul. Did you have a good night?'

He pulled her down and growled in her ear. 'No, I did not. And if we're going to get any breakfast I think we should get dressed and downstairs as fast as possible.' And out of here, he added to himself.

'What, no breakfast in bed?'

'No. Not here. You heard what the man said. But tomorrow morning I'll insist on my favourite breakfast.'

'Oh! What's that?'

'A roll in bed with honey.'

'Oh-ho! Then I think I'll have my favourite supper tonight.'

'What's that?'

'Garlic and syboes sandwiches.'

He smacked her bottom, kissed her and pushed back the bed-clothes. The room was so cold that moisture had frozen on the inside of the window-panes. On the outside ice patterns simu-lated fern leaves, glittering in the pale-red rays of the sun slanting in the left-hand windows.

He looked out on a bleak white wilderness. The snow had ceased falling, having covered the landscape – ground, bushes, trees, hills. In front of the house the open terrain sloped down-wards, with thickly wooded areas of pine and fir on right and left. About four hundred yards away, the shores of a loch could be seen. From the far shore snow-clad mountains rose.

A movement caught his eye. Down below, before the entrance to the house, four men, well muffled up, were trying to dig away the drifted snow, piled high against the sides and fronts of the four vehicles.

With a shiver he turned from the window. Carol was up and dressing, her activities urged on by the chill of the room. He followed her example.

The oil-lamp had been relit in the hall below. It added its light to the sparse amount of daylight grudgingly allowed to filter through the snow-covered glass dome overhead. As they crossed the bare floorboards to the open dining-room door, warmth met them. Inside, the fire was well ablaze, two large log sections crackling and sparking pleasantly. Used breakfast dishes lay on the big table. Arnold Bourne, in a multi-hued Icelandic sweater and dark-grey slacks, sat drinking coffee. Jeremy Hunt, at the other end of the table, was busy scribbling on a clipboard.

'Ah!' said Bourne. 'Our guests. Good morning.'

Carol thought: He really does have an unpleasantly prying sort of gaze. Hunt rose.

'I'll tell our kitchen staff you're here.'

He left the room by the double door in the far wall.

Bourne's enquiry seemed casual.

'How did you sleep?'

'Very well.'

'It was a fearsomely cold night.' His eyes went to Paul. 'And you, Mr Wilson?'

'I did waken up once or twice. Strange surroundings, I suppose.' He decided to change the subject.

'I saw some of your people shovelling snow from the cars.'

'Yes. We'll have your car ready for you after breakfast. I imagine you're anxious to get on your way.'

'Yes.'

Hunt returned bearing a tray laden with dishes. He was followed by Ann Parish carrying a coffee-pot. The smell of bacon and eggs made the Wilsons realize how hungry they were.

As they exchanged good mornings, Paul thought: She senses or knows something. And then, in a fit of impatience with himself: My God! I'm getting absolutely paranoic about this. It's probably just because she knows we're a honeymoon couple.

The door opened and Harry Fletcher strode in. He pushed the hood of his blue anorak back from his head. He hunched his plump shoulders and shivered in exaggerated fashion.

'B-r-r-r! It really is cold outside. Real brass-monkey soprano weather. Is that fresh coffee, Jeremy?'

'It is. How's it going?'

'Okay. We've dug out the Land-Rover and Meredith's Volvo.' He grinned at the Wilsons. 'And your car. We've almost finished clearing the van. I'll go and tell the others to come in.' He halted at the door. 'I've never seen anything like it. That snow was piled up six feet deep against the side of the van. Incidentally . . . it doesn't look too good. We got a weather forecast on the car radio. More snow coming in late this afternoon. The road report said half the roads in the north-west are blocked. Farmers fearing a high death rate in early lambs.' He pulled his hood over his balding head. 'Well, having delivered my load of good cheer, I'll go get the others.'

Ann Parish looked at the Wilsons.

'Is that cottage of yours in good shape? – weather-tight, with plenty of food and fuel?'

Carol buttered a slice of toast.

'Oh yes. It's really very substantial. And Dad made sure everything was ready for us.'

The door reopened. Pollard and Smith came in, followed by Harry Fletcher and Cliff Swanson. They greeted the Wilsons, helped themselves to coffee. Pollard cupped his hands round his hot coffee cup, his face shining with his exertions outside in the cold air.

'Still going off after breakfast?'

'Yes.'

'I don't want to worry you but you may find the going a bit tricky.'

Paul pushed his cup away.

'We'll go carefully. Well now, if you'll excuse us we'll go and pack up.'

In the bedroom, Carol turned to him.

'You were a bit short with them, weren't you?'

'I just want to get out of here.'

'Are you feeling all right?' He saw concern on her face.

'Yes, of course.' He laughed, swung the case he had snapped shut to the floor. 'I just didn't sleep well.'

She said unthinkingly: 'Never mind, you can get off to bed early tonight.' She caught the expression in his eyes, and broke off. Delightedly he saw her colour heighten, her eyes sparkle before her long dark lashes swept down in confusion.

Downstairs they found Meredith and Joyce Mair talking in the hall. Meredith also looked as if he had slept badly. Joyce Mair wore her red ski-outfit again. Outside, the air seemed just above freezing-point. Ann Parish stood talking to the four men who had completely cleared away the snow from around the van, though the side facing the Wilsons was still covered with an opaque white surface of wind-impacted snow.

Captain Pollard strode across to them.

'I hope you don't mind, but we would really feel a bit easier if we provided an escort for you to your cottage. You know, made sure you got there safely and didn't end up in a drift, miles from anywhere.'

While he went through the motions of protesting and apologizing for the trouble he and Carol were causing them, Paul knew he had to accept the offer. He knew it would have been stupid not to. In truth he felt that the road they had traced on the map the previous night could well provide them with some nasty surprises. And yet he could not help wondering if any motive other than concern for their welfare lay behind the offer. Did they want to make sure they got off the premises, that there *was* a cottage they were going straight to, that there was no telephone or, if there was, that it could be put out of action? He surprised himself by his facility for fabricating a wide variety of such dark suspicions. No, he told himself, there was no doubt that last night had rattled him badly.

The cases were stowed inside. Carol was in the front passenger seat. He closed the door on her and looked up at the house.

It was a substantial Victorian mansion of grey sandstone, probably put up in the middle of the last century when labour and materials were cheap and families were large. There *was* a third storey, at least at the front. As well as the seven-sided room above their bedroom, there was a row of three attic windows set in the slanting black slated roof, the panes molten copper-red in the wintry sunshine. Old servants' quarters, he imagined. He saw a further attic window above the bedroom over the dining-room, but belonging to a room not nearly as large as the seven-sided room.

He was about to walk round the car when he noticed a figure at the window of that room. A tall, burly man, clean-shaven and heavily tanned, stood gazing down at them. He was quite unknown to Paul. He had the immediate sensation of static electricity brushing up the hair on the nape of his neck. So there was someone else, some other member of the group who did not wish to be seen. The thought was followed by another. If one, why not more? The house could conceal a dozen men provided they kept themselves upstairs in those servants' quarters. Meredith and company would keep them supplied with food. But why? For what purpose? He made himself pass round the rear of the Capri, hoping no one had noticed his hesitation. Apparently none had. He opened the driver's door, slid into the seat and risked a last glance upwards. The man had gone.

The engine fired at the second attempt with additional choke. It steadied, he let in the choke and shouted goodbye. Meredith and Fletcher waved. As the car crunched crisply over the white driveway, he saw in the rear mirror the Land-Rover fall in behind.

It was not at all worrisome at first. The car moved smoothly along the slowly descending track through the wood, with just a few inches of snow under its wheels. The bad bit came when they broke out of the wood and turned on to the narrow track that climbed round the steep flank of the mountain. To the left the hill dropped sharply, its uneven boulder and bush-bestrewn slope falling down to a twisting, swollen river. On the other side it rose just as steeply. Even in the summer it would have been quite a scramble descending to the river and climbing the other side. Now, with everything deeply covered with snow and ice, it would have been a miserable and hazardous undertaking.

The road dipped prior to turning round the shoulder of the hill. Paul steered the car downwards in low gear, the car engine whining uneasily at the steepness of the gradient. The shoulder was turned and the gradient steepened. His assessment of the view ahead sent a shot of adrenalin coursing through his body. The road fifty feet ahead was invaded from the right by a ten-foot-high mound of soil and boulders from the almost sheer hillside. Beyond the mound a chaos of splintered planks and beams showed where the avalanche had carried away the wooden bridge over the two-hundred-foot deep gully slashed into the hillside.

He stopped the car and got out. A minute later he was joined by the men from the Land-Rover. Smith was the first to put the situation into words.

'Well, back to the house. There's no way out here.' Paul nodded, turned and trudged back to Carol to break the news to her.

Later, when they had managed the tricky operation of turning the cars on the narrow icy road, he followed the Land-Rover back along the track. What were they going to do now? The thought of another night in that icy bedroom or of spending any more time at all in that ghastly house repelled him. Who were these people? He was still speculating uneasily when the vehicles drew up before the pillared entrance to the house.

They got out reluctantly. Apart from the change to daylight, it was a depressing re-enactment of their arrival the previous night. Paul collected their cases from the Capri. Carol shut the tailgate. Pollard, reddish hair dotted with white flakes of snow, came over from the Land-Rover.

'Come in and we'll have a council of war. And some coffee.'

The huge hall was a shade warmer than before, though no more cheerful. The door to the left was open and it was through this opening that Meredith came. He halted, patently astonished to see the Wilsons.

'Good heavens! Couldn't you get through?'

'I'm afraid we're in trouble,' said Pollard. 'The bridge on the hill road has gone.'

'Gone?'

'Landslide carried it away. Must have happened last night. Possibly just after these people came over it. I'd guess the heavy rain followed by the snow set off an earth slip.'

Meredith's forefinger settled his glasses on the bridge of his nose. He ran a hand through his thick, tousled grey-brown hair.

'Then we really are in trouble. For there's no other way out.'

5 The House's Story

They sat in the lounge round the fire, coffee-cups in hand, Paul, Carol, Meredith, Bourne, Hunt and Captain Pollard. The huge room, high-ceilinged, with old-fashioned leather sofas on either side of the fire, and three down-at-heel armchairs before it in an arc, was as depressingly dingy as the dining-room.

Through the windows they could see the ferocity with which the rising wind dashed its white shock-troops against the panes of glass.

The cars will be getting buried again, Paul thought gloomily. As if it mattered. A careful consultation of the map had shown that the road they had tried to follow that morning was the only one a car could use. Meredith had pointed out the peculiar isolation of the house, a combination of its location and the depopulation of the area since the First World War. Roughly speaking, Ardvreck House was set in a semicircle of land sloping down to the rocky shores of the sea-loch which formed the straight part of the boundary. The hills, rising steeply to almost two thousand feet all around, formed the half-circle girdling the area. A spur of almost sheer rock five hundred feet high jutted out into the waters of the loch to the west.

They had reckoned that the nearest inhabited house was ten miles away by straight line almost due north. If one crossed the mountains and kept to the easiest route, it would be nearer thirteen miles, a tiring but not unpleasant day's journey over the hills, through glens and woods and across several burns. In good weather.

Under present conditions, in poor, almost non-existent visibility in a severe snowstorm, with glens almost certainly blocked with deep drifts, the uneven ground and gullies treacherously concealed, it would be a dangerous journey in the extreme.

'We do not send anyone out unless we have to,' Pollard stated. He glanced round the group, addressed Paul.

'Is there a telephone in your cottage?'

Paul, caught on the hop, hesitated. Carol came quickly to his aid.

'No, I'm afraid not. It never seemed worth while putting it in.'

'So it's no use expecting anyone to phone you, get no reply and begin worrying. How soon were you expected back?'

'A week from now.'

'No one in the vicinity will check the cottage to see if you've arrived safely?'

'No.'

Bourne's sardonic face registered a tinge of amusement. His cultivated voice was almost patronizing in tone.

'It does look as if we are caught here until either the weather lifts and we can send someone out or until the outside world notices our continued absence and makes enquiries. It seems to me therefore that we should estimate the minimum likely number of days we are going to have to depend upon our resources and plan accordingly.'

'Not the minimum,' said Meredith, 'the maximum. I've seen this weather last ten days at this time up here. No. No one from Benmore House is going to get worried about us for at least a week. They know we're not on the phone and that we had scheduled a stay of that length of time here. What about your lot, Hunt?'

He shrugged. 'Much the same.'

'And your people, Pollard?'

'We're due back in four days' time. They'll give us a couple of days' grace before they start making enquiries.'

Meredith nodded.

'Well, that's it. We could be here for at least a week before anyone gets worried. Fortunately we came loaded with a week's supply of food. We have calor gas, paraffin for the lamps and there's a log-pile at the rear of the house. Oh, and in one of the cellars there's actually a few hundredweight of coal.'

Hunt drained his cup.

'Well, there's no worry. We can still keep to our previous schedule. In fact from our point of view this weather adds to it. Tremendous atmosphere.'

'I would suggest,' said Pollard, 'that if in three days' time there's no improvement to the weather, we ration our supplies and begin to make preparations to send two of our number out.'

'Like Noah sending the birds out of the Ark,' said Bourne. 'At least it'll be some time before we draw lots to see which of us is eaten first.'

Meredith glanced impatiently at him before turning to the Wilsons.

'I am very much afraid that you seem to be stuck with us. It goes without saying that we will try to make your stay as comfortable as possible but' – he raised both hands, indicating their surroundings – 'it cannot be other than pretty grim for you. I'm sorry.'

Bourne said insistently: 'I really do feel you should put them in the picture, Meredith. Don't you think it's unwise not to – if what you believe is true?'

To his surprise, Paul saw palpable worry and indecision – and something else? – cloud Meredith's fleshy features. He removed his glasses, rubbed one eye as if to gain time, drew in a deep breath and sighed. He replaced his spectacles.

'All right. I suppose if our friends are going to be staying with us, we should try to satisfy the undoubted curiosity they must have felt at meeting such a motley crew in this house.'

Bourne rose.

'Good. Then Jeremy and I will leave you to get on with it. We've heard it all before.'

As they left, Pollard said: 'Do you mind if I stay? I only got the vaguest outline when we were told you'd be here this week.'

'By all means.' Meredith looked at them, hesitated.

Carol thought: Either he doesn't know how to begin or he is not at all sure if we'll believe him. What on earth is he going to tell us?

'Perhaps the best way I can begin is to tell you a little of the history of Ardvreck House.

'It was built in eighteen-fifty-nine by a Glasgow tobacco merchant as a summer residence for himself and his family. He was a keen sailor and loved to spend part of the summer exploring the Western Isles – Mull, Skye, Harris, Lewis and so on. Although

Townsend's main house was in Glasgow, he often lived at Ard-vreck House, entertaining lavishly.

'He seems to have been a bit of an eccentric, being very fond of dogs. He declared that when he died he would return in the body of his favourite dog, a golden retriever. His heir saw to it that there would be no chance of that, for he personally shot all the dogs living at Ardvreck. Nevertheless he was not long here before he took a strong dislike to the place and rented it to a cer-tain Arthur Bertram Howard.

'He took it for the summer of the year eighteen-eighty-eight. According to the records he brought his wife, their two children – a boy of six and girl of two, a governess, a secretary, a cook, coachman, manservant and three maidservants with him. A typi-cal well-to-do Victorian household. Like the late Mr Townsend, he entertained lavishly, with parties of friends from England being invited to stay.

'Howard was a bad lot. He had had the benefits of a good education – Rugby and Oxford – and had entered the diplomatic service but after his marriage he resigned. Anyway, he rented Ardvreck House from Mr Townsend's heir in May of the year eighteen-eighty-eight and came north with his entourage in June of that year.

'The summer seems to have been a success. Howard, strangely enough, seems to have liked the wild beauty and loneliness of this part of the world. His wife hated it. Or rather she hated his hard drinking, arrogance and other things too. She was also lonely. She, I am sure, must have felt despair when he announced that he had persuaded the owner to sell the estate.

'In eighteen-ninety-one Mrs Howard died – of an overdose of laudanum, seemingly. She had been taking it for neuralgia, to help her sleep. To the officer sent from Inverness to investigate the sudden death, Mr Howard, very cut up about his tragic loss, hinted at suicide, rather than accident. That was a mistake on his part. He said he had been worried about his wife's state of mind for some time. She had suffered from fits of severe depression and melancholia. His secretary and manservant, when questioned, confirmed this. Mrs Howard's personal maid said her mistress had never got over her last two babies' deaths before the age of six weeks and had expressed a desire to "join them in heaven".

'A post-mortem was ordered by the Procurator-Fiscal, the description of Mrs Howard's last agonies being decidedly inconsistent with the effects of an overdose of laudanum. The post-mortem revealed Mrs Howard had died of antimony poisoning, no less than forty grains having been absorbed in the form of tartar emetic, a substance readily soluble in water and almost completely tasteless. A dreadful death. This was a different kettle of fish and the upshot was that Howard was arrested for murder.

'The Crown must have believed it had a completely watertight case. Motive? Howard not only had almost got through the money his wife had brought to him on their marriage but he had taken out two years previously a fifty-thousand pounds' policy on Mrs Howard's life. Opportunity? The Crown could show that, in India, Howard had experimented with hashish and other drugs. Indeed, Howard admitted to having a small supply of such drugs at Ardvreck House. As curios. Of course he kept them locked up. But his wife knew where they were kept. But was it likely that Mrs Howard would have taken that way out? She could have simply taken an overdose of laudanum or drowned herself if she wanted to commit suicide.

'The trial was held in the High Court of Justiciary in Edinburgh, opening on Tuesday, first December eighteen-ninety-one. The proceedings lasted a fortnight or so. Howard had a capable defence, not only in his counsel's first-rate brain and wide experience of the law but in his histrionic ability and consummate knowledge of human nature. The Solicitor General, who led the prosecution, was no mean advocate himself but was outclassed.

'From the beginning defence counsel worked to cast into the minds of the jurymen that shadow of reasonable doubt that would prevent them from arriving at a verdict of guilty! William Roughead, genius of crime reporters, wrote of how defence counsel proceeded, "contesting each foot of the ground, plausible, persuasive, with an explanation for anything suspicious, enveloping the plainest facts in an atmosphere of fog – a great performance". The witnesses for the defence, the secretary George Adams, the manservant William Metcalfe and the dead woman's personal maid, Mary Elizabeth Rolfe, were unshakable in their assertions regarding the state of Mrs Howard's mind and her declarations that she wanted to quit this plane of existence.

'As for Howard himself, he bore himself steadfastly throughout the trial. A photograph of him shows a tall, well-groomed man with clean-cut aquiline features and a seemingly sensitive mouth. He was aged thirty-five at the time of the trial and always appeared composed yet – it goes without saying – interested in all that transpired. When anything amusing was said, which, of course, can happen in real life in the most dramatic and deadly circumstances as well as in black comedy, he would be seen to smile, not broadly but rather sadly, as if the irony of the incident had not escaped him even in his tragic circumstances. The truest picture of Howard's mentality, however, comes from the memoirs of the man who attended the trial in the capacity of correspondent of the *Scotsman* newspaper. He wrote:

' "By the time the jurors had retired to consider their verdict, we, hardened pressmen no less than the ordinary spectators, were enthralled by what we had witnessed and sat, conscious of the further drama now being enacted behind the closed doors of the jury-room where Arthur Howard's life hung in the balance. To our astonishment, the accused stood up, turned round and smiled broadly at Vickers of the *Daily Mail* and myself. Howard stretched himself, then indicated the hard wooden bench he had been sitting on. 'Why,' he said, 'am I like a railway engine? Answer: because I've got a tender behind.' " '

Meredith paused.

'The cracking of this schoolboy joke at such a moment, indicating his arrogant confidence and insensitivity, was quite characteristic of the man. Well ... the jury returned after one hour forty-two minutes. The verdict was the Scots one of "not proven". His counsel had managed to instil that reasonable doubt in the minds of the jurymen. Howard rose in the dock, glanced round the court as much as to say "What else?" and bent forward to shake hands with his counsel. The two juniors shook hands with him, but his chief counsel for the defence, it was noted, avoided doing so. Perhaps he had less doubt than the jury.

'That same day, Friday, eleventh December eighteen-ninety-one, Howard, his secretary and those other members of his household who had testified, came back here.' Meredith let his eyes roam slowly round the big dilapidated room. 'One wonders what happened. It was scarcely an occasion for celebration – after all, Howard by all convention was still in mourning for his wife and there was always the well-known cynical sneer to be attached to that Scots verdict of "not proven" – "you've been found 'not guilty' but don't do it again!" '

The Wilsons found themselves speculating on the events of that December day so long ago when the acquitted man and his employees returned to Ardvreck House. Carol tried to visualize the heavy, overcrowded late Victorian décor, ornaments every-where, walls covered with pictures in ornate frames, gas-light hissing gently – would there be gas up here? She didn't know. Paul, intrigued by Meredith's story, wondered what its relevance was.

'They settled down as before,' Meredith continued. 'Or not as before. The two children were sent to stay with relatives of their mother in Shropshire. They never came back. There was a second unfortunate incident six months later when a maid, the Mary Elizabeth Rolfe who had testified at the trial, was drowned in a boating accident. This time it was accepted as accidental death. Various changes were made in the staff over the next year. Parties of people – cronies and business friends of Howard – stayed at Ardvreck House. Locally, the establishment acquired a bad repu-tation. Latterly, none of the people around here would work for Howard – or allow their daughters or wives to go into service. There were stories of drunken parties and worse. Howard, his secretary and his manservant spent a good fraction of the year in London, where he attended to his business interests.

'Ostensibly he was an insurance and financial agent, with an office in Shaftesbury Avenue. In fact he was in league with a number of moneylenders. With his unparalleled knowledge of the seamier side of London Howard would look out for young men who were expecting large sums of money from aged rela-tives on the decease of said relatives. By reason of their predilec-tion for a gay life, however, they were usually hard-up or in debt. Howard would befriend them, advance them money, encourage them to excesses of drugs, drink and debauchery that ran up even larger debts and then introduce them to his generous friends who would make the youngsters an allowance. As security, they had to sign over their expectations. Purely a formality.

'In a number of cases he insured the lives of his protégés for large sums – again as security. There is some evidence to suppose that in the case of two of these young men, who had ruined their health by drugs, Howard managed to substitute his secretary for them when a medical was asked for. And in three cases the youths seemed to die in unfortunate but purely accidental circumstances within two years of meeting Howard.

'On occasion he persuaded his young friends to stay with him here at Ardvreck House. He could offer them entertainment amid the fresh healthy air of the West Highlands. Somehow it didn't seem to do their health much good. One died soon after he returned to London. Another drowned in the loch here.'

Meredith resettled his glasses on his nose.

'And then it all came to an end. Howard, his secretary Adams, and manservant Metcalfe, simply disappeared. They had been here for some weeks in August eighteen-ninety-five. Their few remaining servants, when questioned by the police, said that they had been told by Howard to take one month's holiday with pay. They did so, leaving by hired carriage for Fort William.

'Four weeks later they returned. The front door was locked. The house was uninhabited. There was no sign of Howard, Adams or Metcalfe. Suitcases and clothes had been taken. The family coach and horses were missing. The police were called in, of course, and, rather late in the day, a nation-wide search was begun, with ports being watched for the missing men. For it seemed that the authorities were anxious to have words with Messrs Howard, Adams and Metcalfe in connection with certain insurance swindles, not to mention a number of deaths in suspicious circumstances both here and in London.

'But if the mills of the Victorian police ground as slowly as the mills of God, then in this case they ground too slowly. Howard and his associates got away. Perhaps they had got wind of the coming storm and made their plans accordingly, setting sail for the New World, or even for the colonies, those havens for the misunderstood Briton. In any event they were never seen again.

'In due course the Howard children's guardians applied to the courts to declare Howard deceased, Ardvreck House was sold and thereafter passed through a number of hands. Up until the early twenties there was always someone with money enough to buy the estate but somehow no one stayed more than a few years. It was still difficult to employ local people and as the area became depopulated, especially in the twenties, it became downright impossible. And the turnover in staff was even more rapid than in owners.

'In my researches,' Meredith continued, 'I found that in thirty years two owners and five servants committed suicide. And just before the First World War the London Psychical Research Society sent members to investigate reports by the owner, Sir Henry Fraser, that he and his family and various guests were being troubled by what we would now call paranormal occurrences.'

'You mean "ghosts"?' said Pollard.

Meredith frowned.

'I don't like that term. It's emotive and imprecise. Anyway, according to Sir Henry the phenomena began some months after he and his family took up residence. At first the parents were inclined to attribute them to practical jokes by their children or a member of their staff.

'For example, one morning when Sir Henry and Lady Fraser got up to dress it was found that in a dressing-table in their bedroom every garment was soaking wet. Several days later the same dressing-table was discovered standing two feet out from the wall. On another occasion late one evening after they had retired to bed there was a banging at their bedroom door, so loud and reverberating that they immediately assumed someone was coming to tell them of an accident to or sudden illness of their children or even that a fire had broken out. They lay startled, before Sir Henry called out to whoever it was to enter. No one did. They got up to investigate and found no one outside. And no member of the household admitted banging on the door.

'On several occasions the dining-room table, when set for dinner, would be discovered by a servant to have been rearranged. Knives, forks and spoons would be in the same setting but on the floor round the table, while each chair would be standing on the table as if it had been lifted up and put on the table.

'Chambermaids would make the beds and on reentering the bedrooms, perhaps even only minutes later, find the bedclothes rumpled up or skilfully arranged to give the eerie impression of a person asleep in the bed.

'And in the kitchen, cups and saucers would be found scattered on the floor, unbroken.

'Of course, a watch was kept. Traps were set, but without success. Nothing happened during the time a room was under surveillance. But it only had to be vacated for a few minutes and some phenomenon happened.'

'Wait a moment,' said Pollard. 'I've heard of this sort of thing. Isn't there usually an adolescent involved?'

'In many cases, yes. And in this case two of the Frasers' four children were in their early teens. But it can't have been as simple as that.'

'Why not?'

'Well, in the usual poltergeist case there may be all the phenomena I've already described – and more. But they don't usually go beyond what one might describe as pointless, inexplicable practical jokes, slightly malicious in intent.'

'Do you mean that this adolescent plays these tricks to relieve his feelings?' Carol asked.

'I'm not sure how I should put it,' Meredith admitted. 'It seems that whatever agency in the young person is responsible, it inhabits the deep subconscious. And can control forces that enable its tricks to be carried out. The adolescent may be as scared as any other member of the household.

'No, the phenomena went beyond the usual poltergeist repertoire. One night the youngest child, aged seven, a boy, came screaming into his parents' bedroom. When they calmed him down he sobbed out a story of how he found himself in the cellars of the house. Something terrible – a monster – had tried to strangle him. He fled through the house, up the stairs to his parents' room with it scrabbling after him.

'Of course, the parents thought he had had a nightmare. They sent those members of the household who had been aroused by the little boy's screams back to bed and let their son sleep between them for the rest of the night. But in the morning, in the clear light of day, they saw the smudges on his nightshirt, the dirt on his feet and the purple bruises on his neck.'

Carol, eyes wide, said: 'You mean to say that there really had been an attack on the child!'

'It looked like it. Taken in isolation, of course, it was not necessarily paranormal. But other incidents occurred. A maid told how she had been wakened in the night by a feeling of intense cold. The bedclothes had been stripped from her and a dark figure stood beside the bed. She said she was so paralysed with terror that she could not scream. After what seemed an eternity, the figure drifted away and disappeared. She fainted.

'When she told the cook in the morning, that person, who appears to have been a hard-headed woman, questioned her. She seems to have been satisfied that it was not hysteria and told Sir Henry. The maid was allowed to sleep with another maid thereafter. The cook herself began sleeping in the former maid's room. Within a week she told the Frasers that she had had the same experience.

'The cook claimed that the dark figure exuded such an aura of power and hate that she felt absolutely helpless.' Meredith smiled grimly. 'After that she returned to her former room. It was noticed,' he added dryly, 'that the maids showed a decided tendency to go about their work in pairs whenever possible.' Just as Meredith's people do, Carol thought, feeling her uneasiness deepen.

'There were other disturbing incidents and, as I've said, Sir Henry reported the matter to the London Psychical Research Society. They sent three of their officials – two men and a woman – to investigate. They agreed to stay for two weeks in Ardvreck House as the guests of Sir Henry. The visit was in July. Sir Henry's eldest son Alexander was a student at Edinburgh University at the time. With all the arrogance of youth he believed that there was nothing paranormal in it, that someone was playing tricks, that he and some of his university friends could be more successful than these spook-catchers. And so during part of July nineteen-fourteen there were four sets of interested people in this house – the family, the servants, the psychical researchers and Alexander

Fraser's three university undergraduate friends. I have no doubt they got on each other's nerves.

'For almost a week, as often happens in such cases, the influx of newcomers seems to have inhibited phenomena.' Meredith smiled. 'Parapsychologists are well-used to this. There's an old adage "A watched kettle never boils". Well, the analogous saying in psychical research is "A watched ghost never walks".

'As might be expected, the undergraduates got bored with their unproductive vigil. They were also contemptuous of the methods of the visitors from London, measuring, sealing rooms with blobs of red wax, drawing chalk lines round the objects alleged to have moved, and so on. The psychical researchers also seemed unappreciative of the students' co-operation. In particular the woman, Miss Diana Spencer-Brown, riled them. Going by photographs of the time, she would be about thirty years of age, not unattractive, not unintelligent if one reads the reports she compiled or her other literary works. She was, however, a snob, an inveterate name-dropper and would undoubtedly have tried to impress the household whenever possible with her connections to various English titled families.

'And so two at least of the students concocted a practical joke. Late one night, when it was the turn of Miss Spencer-Brown and Mark Tarrant (one of the students) to be on watch in the gallery, Bernard Gray, the other student, hid upstairs in one of the attic rooms which was alleged to be the place where a number of nasty things had occurred. He had supplied himself with a sheet or something of the sort. The students' brilliant plan was that Tarrant should pretend to hear raps from upstairs. He and Miss Spencer-Brown would then ascend the stairs to the attic room to investigate, whereupon Gray would make noises. The only light would be the oil-lamp Tarrant was holding. When they opened the door, Gray, suitably enveloped in his white sheet, would rear up making spectral sounds, waving his arms, before dashing towards and past Miss Spencer-Brown. Doubtless she would be petrified, giving Gray time to get rid of his ghostly apparel and reach his bedroom.'

Meredith's fleshy face registered anger and his voice hardened. 'It was, of course, a stupid, cruel and totally irresponsible prank. A moment's thought on their part should have led them to discard it as soon as it was suggested. But they didn't. At the appointed time, Tarrant "heard" his noises and led Miss Spencer-Brown up to the attic room.'

Paul, his stomach taut, wondered if it had been the seven-sided room or one of the others. He pictured the young man and the woman creeping up the narrow steep stair that summer night over sixty years ago, the young man hugging to himself his gleeful anticipation of his companion's come-uppance. And the woman. Was she scared?

'They heard nothing as they reached the top of the stairs. Tarrant said afterwards he thought Gray must have mistaken the time or forgotten he was supposed to produce some encouraging noises. So he assured the woman he could still hear raps, hoping that her imagination would feed on that.

'When they pushed open the door of the room it was in pitch darkness. Tarrant felt tense, anticipating Gray's sudden white-clad figure leaping towards them. But nothing happened. The student, irritated, shone his lamp inside the room, hoping that the illumination, dim as it was, would not be bright enough to show up the fact that it was his friend wearing a white sheet.'

Meredith frowned.

'It was then that they smelled the stench pervading the room, saw something huddled under the octagonal table in the centre of the room. Holding the lamp up higher, they approached, crouched to examine the shape under the table. It was Bernard Gray, in pyjamas, the white sheet crumpled up beside him. He lay on his side, bloodless, chalky face towards them, back bent, his body drawn in to the foetus position, his eyes wide and staring and empty. He was alive but quite beyond anyone's reach.

'When they tried to move him they found he had evacuated both bowels and bladder. He was never able to give any account of what had happened to him. Except that he did whisper, just once: "Mummy, it was so dark . . . so dark."

'He remained in that catatonic state for the next twenty-three years, his mind – if it was still there at all – utterly inaccessible to every effort made to reach him. He died in a hospital for the insane in nineteen-thirty-seven.'

Carol shivered.

'That's horrible. Did they never find out what happened?'

'He couldn't tell them. But since he had been, before the practical joke that backfired, a tough, unimaginative rugby-playing healthy young man, it seems highly unlikely that he had been referring to the ordinary darkness of the room in his one utterance. No. Whatever it was, it was something that unhinged his mind completely.'

Pollard said: 'What was the outcome of the tragedy?'

'The three psychical researchers packed up. Doubtless they too were badly affected by the tragedy. In addition, however, they took exception to the attempt to make them appear as fools. They left, having advised Sir Henry to get rid of the house. One of them went so far as to say he should burn it.

'Well, the First World War broke out the following month. Both Tarrant and Alexander Fraser were killed in it, the former at the First Battle of the Somme, the latter at Jutland. It is ironic to realize that if Bernard Gray had not taken part in that practical joke he would probably also have been killed in action. When one thinks of that terrible vegetative existence in which he survived his contemporaries, one feels it would have been better if he had fallen in that war.

'During the twenties and thirties there were three or four changes of ownership with the house lying empty for long periods of time. The Second World War found it handed over to the army. They used it as part of their network for training commandos.

'Strangely enough the army closed it in early forty-three. I never found out why. It had two spells of occupation after the war, once as a private house and once as a hotel of the quiet, secluded fisherman's retreat type. Needless to say, the hotel failed. Very few guests stayed twice. It was impossible to keep staff. It was sold again. The new owners meant to renovate it and live in it. Somehow they never got round to it and it has lain empty for the past fifteen years.'

He looked at his audience.

'And that, in a highly condensed form, is the story of Ardvreck House.'

6 Playback

'Quite a story,' said Pollard. Paul thought the other man did not know whether to believe it or not. His own reaction was a confused mixture of acceptance and rejection. Meredith's manner was convincing but much of what he had related was so extraordinary it was impossible to take.

'What the property agents call a house with character,' he said. 'But I don't understand your interest, Mr Meredith. You're not the owner, are you?'

'No. I'm not the owner. Nor is Captain Pollard. You might say that Captain Pollard and Sergeant Smith are here to see how best they can take Ardvreck House off the owner's hands.'

Pollard grinned.

'Well, that's one way of putting it. Perfectly true. We are here to decide how best to blow the place up.' His eyes glinted at the Wilsons' expressions. 'True. The owner has given up all hope of ever putting Ardvreck House in order. In these days of high inflation it would bankrupt him even to try. In addition it is so isolated here that it has lost all attraction for him. And maybe,' he added thoughtfully, 'he has boned up on its history and decided to live in something with rather less of an atmosphere. So he called us in. In three weeks' time Smith and I will bring our own squad here, install our charges and, in the immortal words, "light the blue touch-paper and retire immediately". Good practice for our men.'

'But why are you here now?' asked Carol.

'When we learned that Mr Meredith and his friends would be billeted here this week we thought we should seize the chance of having a "recce" – you know, look over the house and select in a leisurely fashion the exact places where the explosives will be most effective. Wouldn't do to cause an almighty and spectacular explosion then find that it had been "full of sound and fury, signifying nothing", with half the house still standing. Red faces all round.'

Before Meredith could continue, Ann Parish entered the lounge.

'We're serving lunch in ten minutes. Mr Hunt and his people have already eaten. They thought they would set up their things in here while you ate. You did say you wanted to begin at three, didn't you?'

'That's right.' Meredith rose. 'Perhaps we should continue our talk over lunch.'

In their bedroom Carol turned to her husband.

'Did you believe all that stuff?'

'I'm not sure. Even if Meredith believes it, it's possible that most of it was due to imagination, or hysteria, or exaggeration.' He dug a towel and sponge-bag from his suitcase. 'Let's see what he has to say over lunch.'

She straightened up from rummaging in her own case.

'All right. I won't be a minute.'

When she had gone, he sat on the edge of the bed, chewing over Meredith's story. It could well be true in so far as it was an account of the history of Ardvreck House. But his purpose in being here with his companions could be utterly divorced from anything to do with the house. If so, his account could be simply a smoke-screen to hide his real objectives from the eyes of the two unexpected guests. Paul remembered the man he had seen at the upper window. Again he wondered if he was the only one hidden away. He got up and went to the window. Outside the heavy flakes fell silently downwards to add their fresh contribution to the white shroud covering the ground.

Lunch was adequate if plain. In answer to Carol's question, Meredith said that Joyce Mair and Ann Parish were cooking the meals. As Carol had surmised, they had brought calor-gas cookers with them. Smith and the other men took it in turns to wash the dishes and keep the fires supplied with fuel.

'Then Paul and I must take our fair share of the work,' Carol stated.

'All right.' Meredith smiled.

'You were going to tell us how you came to be up here, Mr Meredith.'

'Ah yes. Tell me, Mr Wilson, do you know anything about psychical research?'

'Not a thing.'

'What's your own line of work, if I may ask?'

'I'm a stockbroker.'

'H'm. A bit far from my field.'

Carol drank some water.

'Isn't extrasensory perception to do with using card guesses to test if people have telepathic or clairvoyant faculties?'

'That's part of it, Mrs Wilson. But there's a lot more to it than that. Psychical researchers, or parapsychologists, are interested in any phenomena that shed light on the personality of man, that seem to indicate that our so-called hard material world – which incidentally has taken a severe bashing in recent years at the hands of theoretical physicists – is only one facet of reality.

'I am the director of a parapsychological institute situated at Benmore House on the island of Mull. Dr Arnold Bourne here is from the Baird Neurological Research Institute at Bristol. Some time ago he stayed with us on Mull taking part in some of our work.' His face carefully neutral, he looked at Bourne who watched him, a tiny smile on his clever, sarcastic features. It's more than dislike that they have for each other, thought Carol.

'I think it fair to say that Dr Bourne, initially sceptical concerning the whole world of "psi", was so changed in his views by his experiments with some of our subjects, in particular two girls, that he has ever since retained a keen interest in the field.'

'Now, Meredith, don't give the impression that I am an out-and-out believer. I will grant you that in certain limited areas there are indications that there's something worth investigating. But so much is wishful thinking, bad experimental technique or downright fraud.'

'That may be, Bourne, but you wouldn't have joined this project if you thought it was a bus ride to nowhere. However, let's not bore our friends with arguments. The point is that Dr Bourne, while doing research on changes of EEG patterns with altered states of consciousness, came across something rather interesting.'

'I'm sorry,' said Paul. 'You've lost me. What is EEG? And what are "altered states of consciousness"?'

Meredith was seemingly taken aback by this display of ignorance. Bourne, in his slightly down-talking, didactic way, filled the gap.

'EEG stands for "electroencephalogram". In our work at the Baird Neurological Research Institute we find it helps in diagnosis to attach electrodes to the scalp and record on a moving strip of paper the patterns of electrical activity in the brain. Now in recent years we have also recognized that as well as the normal everyday conscious state, there are others.'

'But I thought you were either conscious or unconscious,' Carol interposed. Bourne did not bother to hide his annoyance at being interrupted in mid-lecture by such a fatuous remark.

'No, no. That is a gross over-simplification of the truth. There is everyday consciousness, the mystic state, the hypnotic state, the hypnagogic and hypnopompic, and so on. Anyway, I was engaged in studying the degree of correlation of EEG patterns with various altered states of consciousness. At this particular part of the work I was using three good hypnotic subjects. One part of the technique was to regress the subject in age and see whether there were any interesting changes in his EEG trace. There were not but something else emerged.'

'When Dr Bourne stayed with us on Mull,' Meredith chipped in, 'we were just beginning to consider the same sort of phenomena. Dr Bourne remembered this and very kindly invited me to visit him in Bristol to observe his subject. I was able to dig out a lot of the necessary background material, the history of Ardvreck House and so on. When I realized that much of its history came within the province of psychical research my interest deepened. I made enquiries and found to my dismay that the house was due for demolition and that we would have to hurry if we wished to do anything about it.'

Do what, for heaven's sake? Paul asked himself in exasperation.

'The owner was willing to give us permission to come over here and stay as long as we liked. He of course warned us of the state of the property, how it had lain unoccupied for fifteen years. But Dr Bourne, Mr Hunt and I felt it was worth while to set up this operation, especially since it was the last chance anyone would have of ever staying in Ardvreck House again.'

He glanced at his watch.

'Look, it's ten to three. In order to avoid long and lengthy explanations, let's adjourn to the sitting-room. Mr Hunt and his people have been busy, I hope, and will be almost ready for us. Dishes can wait.'

Paul thought that both men, so dissimilar that they constantly irked each other, were at least united in their eagerness to begin. What? He and Carol followed Meredith out of the dining-room, across the cold hall, so dim it seemed to be lit by sunlight filtered through deep water, and into the lounge. Bourne, Smith and Pollard brought up the rear.

The big lounge was transformed. A bulky camera, on a tripod, stood over by the window bay. It was trained on the fireplace area which was brightly lit by two spot-lamps. They seemed to be battery-powered. Cliff Swanson, his long back bent, was peering into the camera viewfinder while Harry Fletcher ran a tape measure from one of the spotlights to the fireplace. Someone had put a fresh log on the glowing charcoal remains of two others. The slightly damp wood was spitting and sparking.

Jeremy Hunt, clipboard in hand, was surveying the lounge, his back towards the door when they entered. He swung round. 'Just about ready.'

Bourne nodded in satisfaction.

'Excellent. I'll go to the kitchen and fetch Miss Parish and Miss Mair.' He strode out of the room. Meredith's voice was dry, with just a shade of irony, as he addressed the Wilsons and the army men.

'Make yourself comfortable but keep the couch to the left of the fireplace empty. Perhaps I should say a few words about the set-up.

'Dr Bourne has made a name for himself not only as a scientist but also from his regular appearances on television. In fact he first came to us at Benmore House following a programme on extra-sensory perception in the course of which I invited him to see for himself the research work we are engaged in. Ever since then he has retained an interest in the field. The presence of our friends here – ' he gestured towards Hunt and the others ' – is a result of that interest. Bourne is presently working on a series of programmes on *The Exploration of Inner Space*, that is, the mind-brain problem. His television producer was extremely enthusiastic that a TV crew came with us here to film our researches. Oh, here they are!'

Ann Parish, Joyce Mair and Bourne filed in. Carol, seated beside Paul on the couch to the right of the fireplace, thought that Ann displayed a diffidence, almost a reluctance to come forward. Joyce, now wearing a pair of heavy-rimmed glasses, carried a clipboard. Bourne, very much the master of ceremonies, disposed everyone like a general making ready for battle.

'Cameras ready? Good. Ann, will you make yourself comfortable on that couch. Captain Pollard, Sergeant Smith. If you would take these armchairs. How is that, Jeremy? All right for the camera?'

Hunt swung his head, looking from Ann, reclining in a corner of the big couch, to his camera. He nodded. Bourne went and sat beside Ann. He nodded at Hunt, who signed to Fletcher. Joyce picked up a clapperboard, stood in front of the cameras. In a businesslike way she clacked the two hinged bars of wood together and said: 'Ardvreck House, take one.' Quickly she stepped back to leave a clear field from camera to Bourne and Ann. He looked steadily at Ann. His voice was firm, confident, authoritative.

'Now, Ann, as at Bristol you are going to go into a deep hypnotic state on receipt of the usual cue. Are you ready?'

'Yes.'

'Good. Ten, five, nine, four, eight, three, seven, two, six, one. Sleep!'

The young woman's head dipped forward, her body relaxed against the junction of arm and couch back. Her eyes were now closed, her breathing calm and regular, her hands clasped in her lap.

'Ann, you can still hear me, can't you, even although you are going even more deeply into the state?'

'Yes.' Her voice was calm.

'But you can hear no one's voice but mine.' Bourne turned to Meredith.

'She's over.'

Paul thought: surely it's not as simple as that? Where is the flashing light or swinging pendulum of fiction? She can't be hypnotized. It must be a fake. He caught Bourne's eye, began to speak then hesitated. Bourne smiled.

'It's all right, she can't hear you. Ask her something.'

'Miss Parish. Thank you for lunch. Will you let Carol and me wash up.'

The figure on the couch did not stir or reply. Meredith rubbed his chin.

'She will only respond to Dr Bourne. Unless, of course, he were to transfer control to someone else. I do assure you, Mr Wilson, she is fully in the hypnotic state at this moment. Now, Dr Bourne, what do you have in mind?'

'I think at this stage a straightforward regression to establish that we can operate under these new surroundings. Agreed?'

Meredith nodded. Bourne turned his attention to Ann Parish.

'Can you hear me, Ann?'

'Yes.'

'Now I want you to go back to the day of your tenth birthday. It is the morning of your tenth birthday. How old are you?'

'I'm ten.'

The Wilsons looked at each other: the voice was lighter, younger.

'Where are you living?'

'Twelve Chester Road, Ipswich.'

'Who lives with you?'

'My mummy, my daddy, my brother Gordon. Oh – ' with pleased excitement ' – and baby!'

'What is baby's name?'

'Sheila.'

'Is anything specially nice going to happen today?'

'Oh yes. I'm going to have a birthday party. Oh, and Mummy and Daddy have given me a beautiful new dress – a blue one.' Confidentially: 'I'm going to wear it to my party.'

'Good. Now I want you to go back to the day of your fourth birthday. It is the morning of your fourth birthday. How old are you?'

'I am four.'

The voice was now solemnly childlike, with the trace of a lisp.

'What is your name?'

'Ann . . . Margaret . . . Parish.'

'Where do you live?'

'Twelve Chester Road . . . Ipswich!' The last word was spoken in triumph.

'Who lives with you?'

'Mummy . . . Daddy . . . and Go'don.'

'Who is Gordon?'

'He's my big brother!' Proudly.

Bourne nodded to Meredith who said: 'She could be taken further back still – and has been, to a stage where she can give descriptions of the scenes she saw looking out from her pram. She can re-experience and exhibit the pangs of her birth.' He saw the expressions on the Wilsons' faces and hurried on. 'Believe me, Ann is in no way unusual. Any good hypnotic subject can be regressed to babyhood. It really does appear that somewhere every human being stores a complete record, intricately cross-indexed, of every event they have experienced.'

He paused, looked thoughtfully at the relaxed young woman lying seemingly asleep on the couch.

'But what we are going to attempt now goes far beyond that. All right, Dr Bourne.'

'Ann, can you hear me?'

'Yes.' The childish four-year-old was still there.

'Now I want you to go back still further, a long way back, before you were Ann Margaret Parish. Back past nineteen-forty, back past nineteen-thirty . . . Paul saw the young woman take a deep breath almost as if about to make a supreme effort. '. . . back to the year eighteen-eighty-six, to the day of your birthday in that year. It is your birthday in the year eighteen-eighty-six.' Bourne hesitated, then asked with deceptive casualness:

'What is your name?'

And with his hair stirring at the nape of his neck Paul heard the voice of Ann Parish, grown up again, but different, say:

'Mary Elizabeth Rolfe.'

7 Voice from the Past?

'Mary Elizabeth Rolfe.'

The name of the maid of Arthur Howard's wife, who had once lived in this house – and had died here. Paul felt his eyes narrow in perplexity: what were Meredith and Bourne up to? Carol's hand gripped his forearm tightly: she too had caught the significance of the name.

'Is there anything special about today, Mary?' Bourne's voice held a note of triumph, and relief. He nodded in satisfaction to Meredith.

' 'Course there is. It's my birthday.'

'What age are you?'

'Eighteen.' The voice was harder than Ann Parish's normal tones, with a slightly alien, difficult to place accent.

'Where are you staying?'

'Thirty-eight Belgrave Square.'

'London?'

'Of course. Where else?'

'Does your family live there?'

'What! Me family live here? Don't be daft!'

'But you live there, don't you?'

' 'Course I do.'

'Why do you live at Thirty-eight Belgrave Square?'

' 'Cos I'm in service, silly.'

'Whom do you work for?'

'Mr and Mrs Rutherford.'

'Now, Mary, I want you to come forward to the day of your twentieth birthday. What day is it?'

'Wednesday.' A note of scorn in the voice.

'And what is the date?'

'August fifteenth, eighteen-eighty-eight.'

'Where are you staying?'

'Ardvreck House.'

'Are you still in service?'

' 'Course I am.'

'Who is your employer?'

'Mr and Mrs Howard.'

'What is your position?'

'Personal maid to Mrs Howard.' A touch of pride in the voice.

'Do you like Mr and Mrs Howard?'

'They're all right.'

'Who else is here?'

'Well . . . there's young Frank and Jennie.'

'Who are they?'

'Mr and Mrs Howard's children.'

'Anyone else?'

'There's Mr Adams and William . . . William Metcalfe. And Miss Fearn.'

'Who is Miss Fearn?'

'The governess.'

'Do you like her?'

The young woman on the couch laughed shortly. 'Her? Too la-di-da for my liking. She may fool some but she doesn't fool me. She's penny plain but thinks she's tuppence-coloured.'

Meredith held up a hand, palm vertical to Bourne.

'Let's take a short break there for a moment. No doubt Mr and Mrs Wilson have questions they'd like to ask.'

Paul hesitated, his eyes on the couch. Meredith smiled.

'I do assure you, Ann cannot hear you. Nor can Mary. They are only aware of Dr Bourne. Indeed when Ann is brought back and wakened she will remember nothing of what has transpired. I may say that this is by no means the first time we have done this with her, though it is, of course, the first time in Ardvreck House. We are very grateful to Ann for her co-operation. She has agreed to be kept in ignorance of everything as long as we see fit.'

'I see.' Paul felt doubt. 'Who is . . . what is . . . this person Mary?'

'Ah, that's the sixty-four-thousand-dollar question. When Mary first appeared it was as a result of a deliberate search on Dr Bourne's part. He is not the first to investigate the field of regression techniques nor the first to carry a subject back before birth.'

'Back before birth?' Pollard frowned. 'Are you saying that Miss Parish had some kind of existence before birth?'

'No. I am only using the jargon that has arisen in this field. Let me explain. What a number of researchers have found is that if some of their subjects were asked to regress to a date a considerable way before their birth they took on – for want of a better phrase – personalities who claimed to have lived at such a date. Such a personality would provide all sorts of data, name, address, relations, profession, describe events that happened to it. What's more, the personality is consistent. It can be revisited at subsequent hypnotic sessions and re-tested, almost always providing the same traits and life-events. You can take the personality through its life from birth to death just as you can take any good subject under hypnosis from birth pangs to the current date.'

'But what does it mean?' Carol asked.

'We don't know. Is Ann allowing her imagination to run riot? Is she fabricating Mary Elizabeth Rolfe? No. For when she first did this in Bristol and Dr Bourne saw how consistent the Mary Rolfe personality was, he tried to check-up to see if such a person ever existed or if a Mr Rutherford had lived at Thirty-eight Belgrave Square, London. When he found that there had indeed been a family of that name living at that address in eighteen-eighty-six he became very interested. So he tried to check on Arthur Howard, mentioned by "Mary" as living at Ardvreck House in eighteen-eighty-eight.'

'I was rather taken aback when that checked out as well,' said Bourne. 'And rather disappointed.'

'Disappointed?' Neither Carol nor Paul could see why this second confirmation had had that effect.

Meredith smiled.

'Arthur Howard was relatively famous in the annals of crime. He had been acquitted on a charge of murdering his wife, been sought by the police in connection with insurance swindles and certain sudden if convenient deaths. And had disappeared without trace thus successfully evading the course of justice.'

'But I still don't see – '

'Ann may at some time in her life have read of the case of Arthur Howard and forgotten consciously that she had done so. In the hypnotic state, with her greatly enhanced powers of recollection, she could be recapturing that data, dramatizing it and acting out the role of Mary Rolfe. Such presentation of information, once memorized but subsequently forgotten, is not unknown. There's even a name for it – cryptomnesia.'

Pollard frowned.

'Do you believe that in this case?'

'Well, not really. There's too much additional evidence. But one must keep an open mind. Anyway, at this point, Dr Bourne got in touch with me and I was able to give him another surprise, namely, that Ardvreck House also occupies a famous place in the annals of psychical research.'

'The Bernard Gray case?'

Meredith's face was sombre in expression.

'Yes, the Bernard Gray case.' He looked at the hypnotized young woman. 'So we decided that we would try to devise some means of testing the cryptomnesia theory. If that could be disposed of, then we would be free to consider the other possibilities more closely.'

For the first time Sergeant Smith spoke.

'Other possibilities?'

'Yes, Sergeant. For example, that Ann Parish in a previous life *was* Mary Elizabeth Rolfe.'

'But ... You mean reincarnation?' The disbelief in Smith's voice was patent. 'You don't go for that old superstitious rubbish. When you're dead, you're dead.'

'Possibly. Possibly not. Believe me, when you've spent as many years in parapsychology as I have, you find yourself forced to consider some very strange concepts with respect to man's personality. And one that has to be treated as a serious possibility is that of reincarnation. I would recommend you, all of you, to read Dr Ian Stevenson's book *Twenty Cases Suggestive of Reincarnation.* And Jeffrey Iverson's *More Lives Than One.* However, perhaps we should continue, Dr Bourne.'

The other man leant forward a little.

'Mary, are you still there?'

'Yes.' The slightly pert voice was as firm as ever.

'What date is it?'

'August fifteenth, eighteen-eighty-eight.'

'I want you to go forward to the evening of December eleventh, eighteen-ninety one.'

With a start Paul recalled that it was the date Howard was acquitted.

'Where are you?'

'Ardvreck House.'

'Has anything special happened today?'

The even breathing quickened a little, a slight flush invaded the cheeks. The tip of her tongue ran round the red lips.

'We're back home.'

'Where have you been?'

'Edinburgh.'

'What was happening there?'

'The trial.'

'What trial?'

'His trial.'

'Who is he?'

'Him. The master. Mr Howard.'

'What was he accused of?'

There was a definite hesitation now, a reluctance to answer.

'Murder.'

'Who was he accused of killing?'

'Her. The mistress.'

'Mrs Howard?'

' 'Course. Who else?'

'What was the verdict?'

'N-not proven.' And with a note of triumph. 'He got off!'

'Are you glad?'

' 'Course I am.'

'Now I want you to go on to the year eighteen-ninety-four. It is your birthday in the year eighteen-ninety-four. Where are you?'

There was silence. Bourne repeated the question but there was no reply. He changed the question.

'Tell me what you see?'

The voice was a whisper, like that of a lost child talking to itself.

'Nothing. It's black. I see nothing. I am nothing.'

'As far as we know,' Meredith commented quietly, 'Mary Rolfe died in eighteen-ninety-two.'

There was agitation visible now in the face of the young woman. She began to breathe jerkily. Bourne leant forward and laid his hand on her brow.

'It's all right, Mary. It's all right. Now I want you to go a long way forward, past nineteen-hundred, past nineteen-forty, to the time when you are Ann Parish. You are Ann Parish, aged twenty-six. You are going to wake up feeling rested, refreshed and relaxed by the time I have counted up to ten. One, two, three – you are beginning to waken – four, five, six – you are becoming conscious again – seven, eight – you are almost alert – nine, ten! Wake up!'

She sighed, opened her eyes, smiled.

Bourne said: 'How are you?'

'Fine. I've had a lovely sleep.' She looked at the dark man.

'Was everything all right?'

'Everything was fine. Thank you.' Bourne turned to the other occupants of the room. 'May I please remind you that Miss Parish has agreed to be kept in the dark regarding anything connected with what we've just heard. In fact, Ann, if you would be so kind as to leave the room . . .'

Good-naturedly, Ann Parish stood up. She smiled at Carol.

'Don't worry, Mrs Wilson, I'm used to being sent out of the room like a naughty schoolgirl. I must confess to being extremely curious about it all but Dr Bourne assures me it's in a good cause and that he will reveal all at the proper time.' At the door she paused. 'I'll get on with the dishes.'

Meredith rose. 'I haven't washed a dirty dish since we arrived, I'll come with you.'

Carol thought: In pairs again – or is he keeping an eye on her to make sure she doesn't listen at the door?

By now the camera had been switched off. Bourne re-emphasized the stricture on communicating with Ann.

'No names of former inhabitants of the house, no history, no discussion of what we are doing. It's vitally important – '

The lounge door reopened. Meredith came in, with Ann close behind him. Her face was troubled. Meredith's expression was unreadable.

'I would like you all to come into the dining-room.'

Something in his tone of voice brought obedience without his listeners doing more than glancing questioningly at each other. He led the way across the dingy hall. They filed into the other room. Paul, entering after Carol, saw those who had preceded him glance round, then up. He heard gasps emitted from Joyce Mair and Jeremy Hunt. When he entered the big room he halted, bumping into Carol, who had stopped immediately she could see what the others had seen.

Each of the long, threadbare, mud-brown window curtains in the bay had been tied in a huge knot. Scattered over the faded carpet were scores of pieces of coal. The two big sideboard drawers had been placed under the table: into the gaps left by their absence, long cushions from the window seat had been stuffed. And on the table, in the middle, a four-foot-high tower had been erected of plates, cups, saucers, two milk-jugs and the coffee-pot, the last balanced precariously on top of the tall erection.

Meredith said quietly: 'Bourne, you brought Ann and Miss Mair from the kitchen. Everything was normal then.'

It was not really a question but Bourne nodded. His eyes flicked over the company.

'And we were all in the lounge. No one left.'

Pollard stared up at the coffee-pot.

'So it must have been done while we were all together.'

Unless, Paul thought, Meredith and Ann set it up then returned to the lounge. But there was not enough time. That tower of dishes must have taken many careful minutes to build. Not to mention taking out the drawers, replacing them with cushions and tying knots in the curtains. And the coals. Don't forget the coals. Unless, his mind skipped on, Bourne, Ann and Joyce Mair did it before they joined us in the lounge. But when he saw Ann's white face, noted the way Joyce Mair nibbled at the side of her forefinger, her eyes, wide in fear, held by the Eiffel tower of dishes, he could not bring himself to buy that one. Someone – Harry Fletcher? – laughed shortly.

'What's it mean?'

'God knows.' The sergeant stepped forward a pace, coals

crunching under his feet. 'Whatever it is, I don't like it. What do you think, Captain?'

Pollard moved his head in perplexity.

'I don't know. A hint, maybe?'

The sergeant compressed his lips. He gestured almost angrily at the curtains.

'You mean, get knotted? Or' – he pointed to the cushions jammed into the holes in the sideboard – 'get stuffed?' He laughed harshly. 'Well, I don't like it. I don't like it one little bit.'

Jeremy Hunt said: 'There's someone else in the house. Someone playing tricks.' His right hand combed his dark beard.

'Don't be ridiculous,' Joyce Mair snapped. 'We would have seen them. And anyway, the doors were locked when we arrived.'

'Well, if there is, they must have spent a hellish cold night,' said Pollard. He frowned, turned to Meredith. 'What do you think? Is it possible there's someone hiding in the house?'

His mouth dry, Paul watched Meredith carefully. On the screen of his mind was projected the image of the man he had seen at the upstairs window. Meredith, obviously worried, hesitated. Quite suddenly, Paul knew beyond any shadow of doubt that whatever was the explanation, he no longer believed that all the people in that room were united in a conspiracy of some sort. Some at least were genuinely puzzled and apprehensive. As if something else was dragging it from him, he found himself saying, slowly and reluctantly:

'There is someone else. I saw him.'

8   Search and Seal

He could not see every face at once to judge their owners' instantaneous reactions. But the general reaction was surprise, or downright astonishment. Alarm, uncertainty, confusion, all these were present. Meredith and Bourne's eyes met. Bourne's incisive, firm voice cut across the initial exclamatory gasps and cries of 'What!', 'Where?'

'You'd better explain, Mr Wilson. When did you see this person?'

Paul described the incident. As he spoke, he could not help noticing how polarized the groups had become. The television people, the two army men, Bourne and Ann, and finally Meredith formed four camps, each seemingly wary of the others. Meredith, his eyes troubled, asked the obvious question.

'Why didn't you tell us this before?'

'I – well, I didn't know why this man was here. For all I knew there was some good reason why he did not appear for meals.'

Pollard scrutinized the occupants of the dining-room.

'I take it no one knows anything of this man?'

No one spoke.

He looked at Meredith.

'Well, what do you make of it? We all met at the house yesterday afternoon. Is it likely that there was an extra man in one of our vehicles? Or that someone was already in the house, concealed, when we arrived? There is that broken window.'

'But why? What's the point?' Ann Parish, perhaps all the more alarmed because of her voluntary ignorance of the situation, glanced questioningly, almost imploringly, at the others. 'What would anyone gain, hiding in this ghastly old house in appallingly cold conditions, coming out to . . . to do this?' Her arm swept out, indicating the bizarre state of the dining-room.

'That we don't know,' Bourne replied slowly, thoughtfully. 'But what I do know is that we must search the house.'

Cliff Swanson nodded. 'We should have done it before.'

'We would have done it last night,' Meredith pointed out, 'if we hadn't been so busy trying to make the place reasonably livable-in.'

Joyce Mair shivered.

'Can't we get this place tidied up first? It gives me the creeps.'

'Not before we've got it on film,' Hunt interjected. 'Okay, Mr Meredith? Dr Bourne?'

They glanced at each other then nodded. Hunt rubbed his hands.

'Fine! Harry, Cliff, set up the camera and lights. Just inside the door for the camera. Dr Meredith. Perhaps you could do the commentary? Joyce: give him a throat-mike.'

Pollard, a trifle impatiently it seemed to Paul, turned to the others.

'All right: I suggest we get out of the way. Let's go back to the lounge. We'll spend the time working out a search plan. When you people have finished, come through. But don't be too long about it. I'd like to get this search carried out before daylight goes completely.'

In the lounge Paul, his arm round Carol's shoulders, sat on the couch they had previously occupied and listened to Pollard, Smith and Bourne thrash out a procedure. The three men sat opposite them, Pollard in the middle, the xeroxed copies of the house plans spread on his knees. The two oil-lamps had been lit to augment the fading daylight. The one on the mantelpiece cast its mellow pool of light over the three men bent over the plans. Ann Parish sat in one of the armchairs, next to Carol.

By now, Harry, Cliff and Joyce had removed their equipment and were presumably recording the manner in which the dining-room had been tampered with. Paul, at one and the same time, listened to the three men and pondered the fact that he had not mentioned to the others the events of the previous night. He realized he felt confused. He knew he still did not trust them all; he wondered if he trusted any of them completely.

At that moment he recognized that he was uneasy at the thought of spending yet another night under this roof, in that freezing cold bedroom. Conscious of Carol's warm shoulders through the fabric of her jersey, he tightened his grasp. She turned her head, smiled slightly, her deep blue eyes meeting his gaze steadily. He smiled in return, squeezed her shoulder again. He caught Ann looking almost sombrely at them and included her in his smile.

From the men's discussion he realized that they were trying to arrange a pairing-up that mixed up the members of the groups – a sign of mutual distrust, he felt – and establish a search procedure that cut out any possibility of the lurker circling round the searchers to cut back into a part of the house already cleared. And in that mode of parallel streams of consciousness sometimes experienced, he heard his own train of thought weigh up the chances of getting a fire going in their bedroom, whether a request for logs and coal would be considered unfair, a needless squandering of the house's stock of fuel, or even, he thought, made from a motive to render the bedroom less off-putting to newly weds. A wave of frustrated desire swept over him and he wished fervently that he and Carol were shot of the lot of them, cosily within their cottage.

'All right then,' Pollard was saying. 'We'll take the floors from the cellars up.' He tapped the paper before them. 'There are two ways up from the cellars. I propose we put people at the top of these stairs while others search the cellar area. Once we've cleared that level, and made sure there's no other way in, we can go over the ground floor. The group coming up into the scullery will search scullery, kitchen and dining-room. Those coming up into the corridor by the butler's pantry will search it, the hall, the lounge, billiards-room and conservatory. We'll keep some people in the hall while this is going on. And,' he added, his gaze going from Bourne to Smith, 'we make sure that all windows are secure. Dr Bourne, can we seal off this conservatory and billiards-room?'

'We can do that. All we need to do is to close that double door between the billiards-room and lounge, nail boards across the doors and put seals on.'

'Good. We'll then tackle the first floor. Having cleared bedrooms three, four, five and seven, and bathrooms one and two, we'll do bedrooms one, two and six, bathroom three and the linen cupboard. Again we make sure that all windows are secure, nailing up any that aren't.'

'I would suggest,' said Bourne, 'that we place threads and seals across all windows, in addition, and across front and back doors even if locked. Even,' he added, 'if we use these doors and it means unlocking, locking and resealing them from time to time.'

Pollard regarded him thoughtfully.

'You mean, in case our friend has a key we know nothing about?'

'Precisely.'

'Look,' Smith asked, 'what's all this business of sealing?'

'It's quite straightforward,' Bourne replied. 'You fasten thread across windows and doors with sealing-wax so that they cannot be opened without breaking the thread or dislodging the seal. The seals are impressed with signet rings so that they cannot be counterfeited.'

'Like this one?' The Captain removed a ring from his finger. He held the gold circlet up, almost as if challenging Bourne.

'Yes,' said Bourne. 'Like that one. And this one,' he added, tapping the ring he wore. 'We'll use both – on each door and window.'

Their eyes met and Paul read their unspoken addendum – and that way there'll be less opportunity for trickery.

Pollard smiled briefly.

'All right. We then tackle the attic floor.' He consulted the plans again. 'There are two stairs to the attics. We go up them, both at once, and work our way along to meet in the middle. And that should do it. If the man you saw, Mr Wilson, is still in the house, we'll find him. And if he's no longer inside, the precautions we'll have taken should keep him out or at least let us know if he comes back in.' Their eyes turned to the windows where flurries of snow still tapped with silent fingers. 'If he can't get in, he can freeze to death or make his presence known by knocking at the door.'

The search and sealing of the house took far longer than they had anticipated. The necessity to ensure that no one doubled round them and that each person's securing of windows and doors was checked by another slowed up the operation.

Descending the flight of stone steps from the bare, peeling scullery into the lower regions of the house was like dropping into an icy black ocean. A miasma of dampness, rotten wood and fungoid dankness touched Paul's nostrils unpleasantly. The torches splashed their light off dirty discoloured brick walls, once whitewashed crumbling stone pillars supporting huge floor beams, unfamiliar dark shapes that turned out to be old chests, or sticks of long-discarded furniture. Down here it was obvious that damp and neglect had worked in collaboration to undermine the stability of the house. Like an elderly, chronically ill person, Ardvreck House existed on the edge of final dissolution. Paul found snatches of property agent's jargon rising in his edgy mind – 'a house with character' . . . 'needs a little attention,' . . . 'splendidly situated in quiet, country surroundings'.

Part of the space under the house was divided into three storerooms, empty now, a wine cellar – the wooden racks were still in position, cobwebbed and dirty – and a fuel cellar. The last place contained a small hill of logs, a pile of coal, grey and dull with its layers of dust, and some drums of paraffin. All these premises occupied the rear half of the available space. The front half of the house basement had never been partitioned. An outcrop of rock over most of the area pushed up to within a metre of the ground floor. Paul and Fletcher, crouched like miners in the dark enclosed space, explored the area before them, their torch beams penetrating to the front of the house or being reflected from the short, massive stone pillars set in the solid rock.

Nothing was found.

Paul recognized the relief he felt when they finally ascended the stone steps to the ground floor. It was understandable in a way but it still worried him. Certainly it was nasty downstairs but he wondered if he was over-reacting, if he perhaps had a thitherto unsuspected tendency to claustrophobia. He remembered the story Meredith had told of the Frasers' youngest child screaming that he had been attacked by a monster in the cellars. If the child had sleepwalked down through the house to the cellar region, and then wakened in that stifling darkness, it was not at all surprising that he had been catapulted into hysterics.

Under Pollard's direction, the groups continued their search. They cleared and sealed the ground floor, with the three women stationed in the hall to cover the stairs. Paul was in the two groups who did the billiards-room and conservatory. The billiards-room doubled as a library. Apart from the full-sized billiards-table occupying the centre of the floor and the rack of cues against one wall, one or two warped with age, the only other furniture consisted of two leather-covered armchairs one on either side of the empty fireplace. Unless one counted the seven-foot-high rows of bookshelves along the outside wall of the room. Huge sections of the rows were devoid of books.

The conservatory, entered from the billiards-room, had probably once been impressive. In the hot, slightly humid atmosphere Victorians doubtless admired dazzling displays of colour from the carefully cultivated plants, sheltered under the roof of glass supported by ornate cast-iron pillars. Even now, with many of the panes of glass missing or shattered, with the bare, rusty pillars standing like winter-struck trees and the earth within the ruin empty of plants and white with snow, Paul could visualize what it must once have looked like. Perhaps Arthur Howard had sat in here on a mellow summer evening, his cigar burning satisfactorily, putting the last touches to his plan to poison his wife and claim her insurance money. Or did he plan it over a quiet game of billiards in the adjoining room? Did he even do it at all? And as they left the billiards room prior to sealing it, Paul wondered: whether he did or did not kill her, did the insurance company pay up? After all he was found not guilty. No. The verdict was 'not proven'. Would that have made any difference? He did not know.

He watched as Sergeant Smith and Harry Fletcher nailed wooden battens across the double doors between lounge and billiards-room, sealing off the rooms beyond.

They went upstairs. The rooms on that floor were searched and secured. Again the women stood on the landing where they could watch the stairs. Again nothing was found. Which left the attic floor. If the man was still in the house, thought Paul, he had to be upstairs. Man, or men, or . . .

Pollard, from the near end of the corridor between bedrooms three and four, called to the women.

'You three stay where you are. Mr Wilson, Mr Fletcher, Sergeant Smith and Dr Bourne take the other staircase. Mr Meredith, Mr Swanson, Mr Hunt come with me.'

Paul found himself following the sergeant up the same narrow, steep flight he had climbed the previous night. Was it a memory of his terror then that squeezed his stomach now, or was it apprehension about meeting a possible lurker or lurkers at the top of the stairs?

Daylight was almost gone now. They had brought oil-lamps upstairs to the first floor gallery and left one burning in the hall below. But on the narrow stair it was so dark they required torches. Even when they reached the top, the pale dusk light filtering through the three dirty windows on the left of the long low passageway ahead did very little to illuminate it.

At the far end they saw the moving torch beams of the other group of searchers. Bourne got to the top of the stairs.

'Sergeant, if you stay here in view of whoever's at the other
end, Wilson, Fletcher and I will do the tower-room.'

Smith nodded abruptly.

The seven-sided tower-room was entered and searched.
Through the uncurtained windows Paul saw the last sad light
over by the western horizon reveal a grey, bleak landscape, icily
forbidding, though surely no colder than the atmosphere of this
room. Paul noted how Bourne hunched his shoulders against the
chill, how Fletcher drew in long, shivering breaths. As quickly as
they could, they finished with it and left, shutting the door behind
them.

They met up with the other group in the corridor, just opposite the big glass dome set in the snow-covered roof. All the
rooms on that floor had been searched and sealed. They were
all empty. Almost certainly servants' quarters in the house's Victorian past, these dingy cramped rooms held trunks, bare iron
bedsteads, cheap chests of drawers, and a large assortment of the
other flotsam that every old house accumulates. Cumbersome
vases and jugs, a row of heavy faded glass-framed photographs –
was Arthur Howard among them, or the unlucky Mrs Howard?
Paul wondered. There was even an old rocking-horse, its harness
tattered, its paint worn away by the loving hands and knees of
long-dead children.

And that was all.

In the narrow corridor they looked at each other. For a long
moment no one spoke.

'Right,' said Pollard, 'let's get back down to the lounge. Mr
Wilson, you and I will take a turn round the house outside if you
don't mind, and look at the cars. Mr Fletcher, Ted. You too. You
go in the opposite direction. After we've checked the cars. Dr
Bourne, Mr Hunt. You let us out and stay by the front door until
we knock to get in again. Okay?'

In the sharp chill outside the snow was deep and powdery
underfoot, almost blue-white in the torchlight. They swept snow
from the car door-locks and made sure no one was inside the
vehicles. As on that morning the cars were almost shapeless again
under their white covering.

If there had been footprints, fresh snow must have obliterated them. The only marks on the surface when they returned to the front door were their own new-made trails.

In the hall, Paul watched Bourne re-lock the door. The ritual of threads stuck over the jamb by blobs of red sealing-wax was enacted with Bourne and Pollard pressing their signet rings into the soft wax.

It was agreed that Fletcher and Smith would restore the dining-room to order while the three women prepared the evening meal. On Pollard's suggestion the others retired to the lounge to discuss the situation. In the big room Hunt threw another log on the fire before sitting down opposite Paul. The other four men disposed themselves in the semicircle of armchairs and sofas.

Pollard ran a hand through his red hair.

'I want to speak bluntly. What are we sure of?

'We are as sure as we can be that we are the only people in the house, as of this moment in time. We are also sure that the curtains and dishes and so on in the dining-room were tampered with. And that is all we are sure of.

'We do not know who did this or why.

'It is possible that it was done by someone who was concealed in the house – Mr Wilson's man? – and has now left, or by one or more of us. If it was us, then the only candidates are Dr Bourne, Miss Parish and Miss Mair who were the last to come to the lounge this afternoon, or Dr Meredith and Miss Parish, who left the lounge before us and ostensibly discovered the rearrangement.'

Meredith, about to speak, was forestalled by Bourne.

'I follow your argument, Captain Pollard, and agree entirely. But I really feel it is beyond credibility that Dr Meredith and Ann arranged the dining-room display. It is my recollection that there just was not enough time for them to do so before they asked us to come through.'

'That's right,' said Swanson. 'I switched off the camera. I remember I just had time enough to note how much film we'd shot when Mr Meredith and Miss Parish came back in.'

Pollard nodded in satisfaction.

'Good. That's what I felt but I wanted to hear it from you, too. Which,' he added slowly, 'brings us to Dr Bourne, Miss Parish and Miss Mair.'

'There wasn't time.' Paul found himself quite sure of that. 'Think about it, Pollard. Think of what we talked about when we came in here after lunch. There just was not enough time for Ann and Joyce, with or without Dr Bourne's help, to set up the dining-room.'

There was silence. He held Pollard's grey eyes for a long moment. The army man sighed.

'All right. I agree . . . So where does that leave us?'

Jeremy Hunt stirred.

'We're back to Mr Wilson's intruder, surely? He must be a nut-case. Maybe a tramp who was sleeping in the house heard us arrive, lay low and then . . .' He broke off, shrugged. 'Doesn't seem likely, does it?'

Meredith spoke for the first time.

'Mr Wilson, are you absolutely sure you saw a man at the upstairs window?'

Startled, Paul recalled the scene.

'Of course I did. The light was good. I saw him distinctly.'

'You could not have been mistaken?'

'No, absolutely not.'

Meredith did not pursue the matter. But Bourne did, a glint of understanding in his sharp eyes.

'Are you thinking Mr Wilson was hallucinating?'

Meredith nodded slowly.

Paul felt annoyance flare within him.

'Hallucinating! Look, I am not subject to hallucinations!'

Meredith made smoothing-down gestures.

'No, no, Mr Wilson, you misunderstand me. I don't mean "hallucinations" in the normal way.'

'Hallucinations in the normal way?' Jeremy Hunt grinned. 'Surely it's abnormal for anyone to suffer hallucinations?'

Meredith, conscious of Bourne's mischievous pleasure in the contretemps, sighed.

'I expressed myself badly. What I was trying to say is that normally we attribute hallucinations to mental disorder due to brain damage or drugs or hypnotic direction. For example Bourne could arrange it that Ann Parish would see an additional person in this room. Such a person's appearance would be totally convincing to her. If that person sat on a chair, he would block out the correct parts of that chair. In other words, within us there is a mechanism that can manufacture or stage-manage a production, animate or inanimate, that can fool us.' He looked at Paul. 'What I was suggesting is that you may have picked up something from this house which triggered-off the hallucination of a man. You see we have to remember its history. I think we have to consider it a distinct possibility that Mr Wilson saw an apparition at that window. Just' – he raised his voice and hand to forestall any reaction – 'as we have to consider that if that was so, there may have been no intruder. And therefore, since we have eliminated the possibility that any of us disturbed the dining-room, it is at least possible that the happening was supernormal.' His face deadly serious, he continued: 'With so many people living in the house again, it may be that it is, for want of a better word, powering-up again.'

9   Echo of a Tragedy

' "Powering-up".' Bourne did not attempt to hide his scorn. 'Not a very scientific term, if I may say so.'

'I know. But there are plenty of cases in the literature of houses where there seems to be a necessity that with a new family in residence some time must elapse before the phenomena – whatever they are – reach a climax.'

Pollard, obviously treading warily on totally unfamiliar ground, frowned.

'But the house has been lying empty for fifteen years. And we've been here just over twenty-four hours. Surely that's a bit too fast for it to be "recharging its batteries"?'

Meredith turned his head and firelight sparked from his glasses.

'That is one of the things that worries me. It is fast. Almost as if . . . well, almost as if whatever it is is aware that this is its last opportunity.'

'Opportunity? For what?' Jeremy Hunt's voice was sharp.

'I don't know. Communication, possibly. I am not trying to alarm you but I feel I must alert you.'

'Well, you're scaring me spitless,' said Hunt, half-facetiously. 'Pollard, if you find me in your bed tonight it won't be because I'm that way' – he bent a wrist limply, 'but just because I've heard clanking chains.'

Paul saw the army captain grin. Bourne's sardonic face took on a look of impatience.

'Well, really, Meredith, I must protest at this utterly unjustified and totally irresponsible speculation. It is not going to help our experiments if we are all going to be looking fearfully over our shoulders for bogeymen.' He looked scathingly round the room. 'I may say that I intend to get as good a night's sleep as is possible in that rather less than five-star bedroom you've put me in.'

Listening to Bourne's acid tones, Paul realized he had arrived at a moment of decision. The bickering discussion, following as it did the long-drawn-out search and painstaking sealing of the house, had finally undermined the suspicion that these people were united in some elaborate hoax to bemuse Carol and himself. He found himself accepting them at face value, three groups, scientists, army men and TV team, met in this age-crazed old house for various reasons.

'Before we go any further,' he said, 'I think there is something else I should tell you.'

'Something else?' Meredith, about to reply to Bourne, shot a questioning glance at Paul.

'Yes. Something that happened last night.'

He had their attention. Slowly at first, reluctantly, he began to recount his experiences of the disturbing noises from the seven-sided room above his bedroom, of how he had gone upstairs to investigate.

'Well,' Hunt breathed. 'I do hand it to you, Wilson. I certainly wouldn't have gone up that stair alone. Weren't you scared?'

'Scared spitless.' Hunt grinned at Paul's use of his own phrase.

Bourne rested his chin in his hand.

'You say these noises were loud?'

'Yes.'

'Yet your wife did not wake?'

'No.'

'Is she normally such a sound sleeper?'

Paul hesitated, cursing himself for doing so. Meredith stirred.

'Remember, Bourne, they'd had a long and tiring journey.'

'Why didn't you wake her?' Bourne pursued.

'Because I felt – well, I saw no reason to. It might have alarmed her.'

'So we have only your word for the whole thing.'

'Y-yes.'

'Like the man you saw at the window.'

Paul felt his face flushing at the tone in Bourne's voice.

'Why didn't you tell us this morning?' Bourne asked. 'You do remember that I asked you if you'd slept well?'

'I do remember.' He found himself gazing almost defiantly round the group. 'But I believed we would be leaving shortly. And –'

'And?' It was Pollard who repeated the word.

'Well – ' He stopped, took a deep breath. 'I simply did not know what was going on. I felt it best . . .' He shrugged. Pollard nodded.

'Felt it best to keep a low profile. Yes. I think it's understandable, Dr Bourne, that he should keep quiet this morning.'

Bourne said nothing. The sceptical look on his face remained.

'Well,' said Pollard. 'I don't know what to suggest. What do you think, Dr Meredith? What's the chance of these noises being heard again tonight? Should we set up some kind of watch system?'

Jeremy Hunt added quickly: 'It'd really be something if we could get them on tape!'

With a crashing sense of dismay Paul suddenly realized the trap he had dug for himself. He saw the other occupants in the house taking it in turn to camp out in their bedroom. Quickly he sought for some way of dissuading them. And as before Meredith came to his aid.

'You're quite right, Captain Pollard. You too, Mr Hunt. We should try to record these phenomena. Nevertheless there's no guarantee that it'll happen again tonight. Apart from that, if we took turns to listen from the Wilsons' bedroom it would mean explaining to Mrs Wilson something of what we were after.'

'We could move them into another bedroom. Isn't bedroom

seven unoccupied?' Paul saw that Pollard seemed to have taken the bit between his teeth.

Meredith shook his head.

'No, that won't do. It would still mean explaining to Mrs Wilson. And in any case, bedroom seven is the one with the smashed window. Although we've boarded it up, it is draughty and icy-cold. No. I suggest we see what transpires tonight. Mr Wilson was wakened by the noises last night. If he is wakened again tonight, he should come and rouse the men.'

'Well,' said Pollard doubtfully, 'if you think that's the best approach tonight.'

'I do. We could spend a whole night watching and get nothing.'

The lounge-door opened and Carol entered. She smiled.

'Gentlemen, dinner is served.'

As they rose, Meredith looked at the other men.

'Let's leave this until after dinner. All right?'

They nodded. They began to drift out of the lounge in pairs. Behind Pollard, Paul saw him turn towards Meredith.

'Do you know what room Bernard Gray was in when he was found?'

The bulky man glanced once towards the door to make sure Carol was out of earshot.

'The tower-room.'

It was a surprisingly pleasant meal at the big table in the dining-room. Unlike the alfresco arrangements of the previous evening, the table was properly set on this occasion. The fire and lamplight co-operated in producing at least an illusion of comfort. Pollard described some of his lighter experiences with NATO forces in Europe. Jeremy Hunt, aided and abetted by Joyce Mair, told a number of wildly slanderous tales about various television personalities they had worked with. Even Bourne, apart from indulging in one or two astringent exchanges with Meredith, seemed more agreeable than before.

Towards the end of the meal, when they were all supplied with coffee, Bourne looked at his watch.

'Eight-forty-five. Do you think we could be ready by nine-thirty to have another session with Ann?'

'I don't see why not,' said Hunt. 'Cliff. Will you and Harry get everything set up in the lounge when you've finished coffee? We'll let you off doing the dishes. I take it you don't mind us getting this on film?'

Bourne shook his head. 'Not at all. Ann, how about you?'

'I don't mind.' She smiled good-naturedly. 'Someday I may even be allowed to watch it.'

It was agreed that Paul and Carol and the two army men would clear away the dinner dishes, wash them, rebuild the fires and check the paraffin levels in the oil-lamps. By nine-thirty they had all assembled in the lounge. From where he sat Paul could see the unpainted battens of wood nailed across the two varnished doors into the billiards-room, the small, scarlet blobs of wax resembling drops of blood. It occurred to him that if the doors now prevented anyone getting in, they also effectively prevented anyone from this side knowing what was happening in the darkness beyond them. Impatient with himself at what he considered to be craven imaginings he steered his attention to the couch opposite where Bourne was inducing Ann into the hypnotic state.

'. . . . seven, two, six, one. Sleep!'

As before, her head dipped, her body relaxed, her eyes closed. She lay back against the corner of the couch, as if in a normal sleep. As on the previous occasion her hands were clasped loosely in her lap.

'Ann, you can still hear me even although you are going deeper and deeper. Can you hear me, Ann?'

'Yes.'

'You can hear me but no one else.'

He looked at the silent semicircle of watchers.

'She's over. You can talk freely now.' He turned to the hypnotized woman. 'I want you to go back in time, Ann, back before nineteen-sixty, back before you were born as the human being who is now Ann Margaret Parish' – Paul saw the woman's head rise and fall as she took in a deep breath – 'back to the year eighteen-eighty-eight to the day of your birthday in that year. It is your birthday in the year eighteen-eighty-eight.' Bourne paused.

'What is your name?'

And again the pert, slightly alien voice they had heard before spoke from Ann Parish's lips.

'Mary Elizabeth Rolfe.'

Something like a collective sigh came from the listeners. Carol's hands gripped her husband's arm and she looked at him, wonder and inquiry apparent on her face.

'What day is it, Mary?'

'Wednesday. *I've told you that before.*'

Shock on his face, Bourne looked at Meredith. The other man's fleshy features also registered surprise.

'She remembered you! Now listen, Bourne, I have wondered about this in our past sessions. Who does this personality think you are? You enter into conversation with her, ask questions. Who does she think you are? How does she fit you in to her world?'

Bourne nodded. He turned back to Ann.

'Do you recall our past conversation, Mary?'

' 'Course I do.'

'On your birthday?'

'Yes, silly. I've got a good memory.'

'Who do you think I am, Mary?'

A frown, then a bright calmness.

'Why, you're one of my dream people.'

'Dream people? What do you mean?'

'Well . . . When I'm day-dreaming I imagine you – and all the others.'

'Do you day-dream a lot, Mary?'

'Oh yes.'

'About what?'

'Oh, about seeing the world. About marrying. Maybe a peer of the realm. Maybe having a nice house of me own. Oh, lots of things. You know . . .'

'Mary, where are you living now?'

'Ardvreck House.'

'Mary, I want you to go forward now to the evening of December eleventh, eighteen-ninety-one. Where are you now?'

'Ardvreck House.'

As on the previous occasion when she had been taken to

the night of the acquittal of Arthur Howard, Ann's breathing speeded up.

'What happened today?'

'His trial finished.'

'Whose trial?'

'The master's. Mr Howard.'

Meredith brought a notebook from his pocket and opened it. He consulted a handwritten entry.

'This is as far as we got in Bristol,' he explained, 'though we did learn that the personality finished that life six months later. Since that session in Bristol we have been occupied in trying to assemble the history of Ardvreck House and its successive occupants. Now we may be able to get a little first-hand information, so to speak.' He nodded to Bourne after showing him the entry in the notebook. Bourne leaned forward.

'Mary, I want you to go forward to the morning of Wednesday, June fifteenth of the year eighteen-ninety-two. It is about ten in the morning. Where are you?'

'In the linen-room with Ethel.'

'What are you doing?'

'Fetching clean linen for the bedrooms.'

Paul frowned. There was something different about the tone of voice. It was flatter, leaden with indifference or unhappiness. Apparently Bourne noticed this as well.

'Are you happy, Mary?'

The woman sighed deeply. He had to repeat the question before he got an answer. When he did there was a tinge of bewilderment and bitterness in the voice.

'Is anyone?'

'Are you worried about anything?'

'I – ' A deep sigh. 'I don't know.' A frown. 'It'll be all right. It'll come all right. He can't – He wouldn't . . . not after . . .' The face hardened into a stubborn expression totally unlike any previous one Paul had seen on Ann's face. His fascination grew as he imagined he could almost see the woman's face change like wax into the cast of another countenance. A long-dead one?

'Tell me about it, Mary.'

'I can't.'

'You can tell me, Mary.' Bourne's tones were persuasive. 'I am here to help you.'

'No. I can't. It is a secret. I can't.' The voice was agitated now; the head moved uneasily, the breathing quickened.

'All right, Mary. Be calm. Be calm.' He frowned. 'Now I want you to go forward to two o'clock on the afternoon of the same day. What is happening?'

'We've just eaten.'

'Where?'

'In the kitchen.'

'What are you going to do?'

'Help to clear up.' The voice was dull again.

'And after that?'

'I've got the afternoon off.' Indifference.

'Are you going anywhere, Mary?'

'Are you joking?' There was a flash of the old pertness. 'There's no place to go round here.'

'What are you going to do then?'

'William's taking me out in the boat.'

'When?'

'At three.'

'Who is William?'

'William Metcalfe. The manservant.'

'Is he fond of you?'

'Yes.' She smiled.

'Are you fond of him?'

'He's all right.' But the answer was given flatly.

'Do you think he'll ask you to marry him?'

'He has.'

'And will you?'

'No.' There was scorn in her voice.

'Why won't you marry William?'

'I can't tell you that.' Firmly.

'All right, Mary. Go forward to three o'clock. Where are you now?'

'I'm at the boathouse.'

'All right. Go forward to half past three. Where are you now?'

'Out in the boat.'

'What kind of boat is it?'

'A sailing-boat.'

'Is it a big one?'

'No. Not very. Just a rowing-boat with sails.'

'Is William with you?'

'Yes.'

'Where is the boat now?'

'Round past Crag Point.'

'Can you see the house from there?'

'No. It's beyond the Crag.'

'Are you enjoying the sail, Mary?'

'It's all right.'

'Does William seem happy?'

'He's quiet. He asked me to marry him again. Said it was my last chance. And I said no.'

Bourne opened his mouth then closed it again. The woman was frowning as if in puzzlement. Her head moved.

'What is happening, Mary? You can tell me. You can speak about it!'

'He's saying I'm a fool!' There were overtones of agitation and surprise. 'He's standing up. Holding on to the mast. He's rocking the boat. Oh God, it's going over. Help! I'm in the water.' Ann's body twitched and jerked on the couch, her hands unclasped and her arms began to flail. 'I'm drowning!' She gasped and choked. 'I'm up again. Waves. William's beside me.' She screamed, gasped. 'Ah-h-h, he's pushing me under.' She struggled wildly, choked, gagged, her face purple. Meredith restrained her convulsively moving arms while Bourne spoke urgently and insistently to her. The others in the room sat rigid with shock.

'You're safe, you are not drowning, you are going into sleep, you are coming forward in time, you are no longer concerned with Mary Rolfe, you are coming forward to the time when you are the person named Ann Margaret Parish. You are becoming Ann Parish. You are Ann Parish again. Rest peacefully. You are relaxed, content and happy. You are perfectly safe.'

The young woman stopped screaming, gradually quietened to become as composed as she had been before she began her frenzied struggles in the water to escape drowning. Paul felt shattered: it had been all too realistic. He glanced at Carol, realized she had been equally shocked. The others showed various degrees of startlement.

Meredith returned to his seat. He retrieved the notebook which had fallen when he leaped forward to restrain Ann. Opening it, he read: ' "At the fatal accident enquiry, the witness William Metcalfe stated that the boat met a sudden gust of wind. Before the occupants could shift position, the boat heeled over and capsized. He did not see Miss Rolfe again though he dived again and again to find her. He even looked under the upturned boat to see if she had been trapped under the sails. But, he said, there was no sign of her!" ' He looked up. ' "Her body was recovered three hours later. The verdict was death by misadventure." '
He rubbed his chin, his eyes on the hypnotized woman. 'Perhaps you'd better bring her out of it, Bourne. She's certainly given us a lot of food for thought. Enough for this evening. Obviously we'll have to discuss our future line of approach before we proceed.'

'Agreed.' Bourne turned to Ann. Giving her the usual suggestions that she would be restored to ordinary consciousness feeling rested, relaxed and refreshed, he wakened her up.

'How do you feel, Ann?'

'Fine.' And indeed she seemed calm and happy.

'Do you remember anything at all of what went on while you were hypnotized.'

She thought for a moment, a slight frown between her dark brows.

'No. Should I?'

Bourne smiled, shook his head.

'No. That's all right. You did very well indeed.' He paused. 'And now – '

She shrugged, sketching exaggerated resignation. 'And now you want me out of the room as usual. Yes?'

'I'm afraid so.'

She stood up.

'All right. I'll go and put on kettles for coffee and for hot-water bottles.'

Carol offered to help her. When they had left the room, Pollard passed round a packet of cigarettes. He lit his own.

'Well, now, what are we to make of all that?'

Meredith closed the notebook.

'Well, there are a number of possibilities that have occurred to us. Accepting that Ann is genuinely hypnotized – and I do – she may be role-taking, that is she may have read an account somewhere of Mary Rolfe and of her death and is now acting it out.'

'But she got it wrong,' Pollard pointed out. 'As far as we know, Mary Rolfe's death was an accident.'

'As far as we know.' Meredith agreed. 'But Ann may have dramatized it.'

'And this,' Pollard said slowly, 'would be the most reasonable explanation.'

'Surely it depends on what you mean as reasonable,' Bourne said. 'If we continue and find that in her state of "Mary Rolfe", Ann provides us with large quantities of information about Ardvreck House and its occupants she could not have acquired normally except by long and painstaking researches in a number of sources, then the cryptomnesia role-taking hypothesis becomes less and less reasonable.'

'What are the other possible theories?' Paul asked.

'Well,' said Meredith, 'there's the reincarnation theory. Is it possible that in a previous life Ann Parish was Mary Elizabeth Rolfe?'

'But where does she get those memories?' Pollard asked. 'Presumably they can't be stored in her brain.'

'Almost certainly not,' Meredith agreed. 'The reincarnation hypothesis implies that "somewhere else", whatever that means, the memories of past lives are stored – and can be tapped. Or is it that she never was Mary Rolfe but has the ability when hypnotized to plug in to the record of the life of Mary Rolfe? If so, why the life of Mary Rolfe? What particularly attracts Ann to the life of this chambermaid who lived in the last half of the nineteenth century? Or does Ann become possessed temporarily by the spirit of Mary Rolfe? Or is she practising clairvoyance or some form of psychometry? Or is there anything in the idea of genetic inheritance of memory from an ancestor?'

He shrugged.

'There are so many possibilities and all of them intriguing.'

Pollard tossed his cigarette into the fire.

'But what do you think of what we got tonight? William Metcalfe was the manservant here. And he was one of the three men who were sought by the police and did a bunk. Do you think he really drowned Mary Rolfe?'

'Who knows?' Meredith removed his spectacles and rubbed his eyes.

'And what about Mary's unhappiness? I got the impression she had changed between the date of the acquittal and the day of her death.' Pollard frowned. 'Of course, as you told us, there had been changes in the household. The children had gone. And the governess. Howard had lost most of his respectable friends. It was probably a pretty grim household by then.'

'Well, perhaps we will learn more tomorrow,' said Meredith. Paul, listening to them, found his gaze wandering round the big dilapidated old lounge. These faded walls had seen much of the drama enacted at Ardvreck House. Was it really the case that houses stored up the scenes they had witnessed as a magnetic tape records song and speech? And if the right instrument is brought – a sensitive human being? – can those bygone people be made to walk and talk again just as the golden voice of Caruso may still thrill a generation half a century after the lungs and larynx that produced it became dead flesh?

He did not know. But what he did know was that he found it difficult not to accept at face value the person claiming to be Mary Rolfe, difficult not to become involved in her troubles, difficult not to want to learn more, if possible, of the events leading to her death by drowning in the year eighteen-ninety-two.

10   Lost One

By the time they had had coffee and cleared away it was eleven-thirty. Paul and Carol wished the others good-night and left the lounge. As they climbed the stairs, their oil-lamps lighting the darkness, Carol said:

'So much for our early night.'

'So much for our cottage.'

The room was almost as icy as on the previous night. Paul had left the bedroom door open earlier in the evening in the hope that heat rising from the lounge and dining-room would alleviate the chill. It did not seem to have worked.

'I wrapped our pyjamas round the bottles,' said Carol. She picked up her housecoat, her toilet things and an oil-lamp. 'Let me use the bathroom first. I'll try not to be long.'

When she had gone, he sat on the edge of the bed, his hands thrust in his trousers pockets and wondered how on earth Eskimos managed it in their igloos. The cold air began to reach him through his heavy sweater and he brought one of the old-fashioned stone hot-water bottles from under the blankets to hold in his lap. Occasionally he found his head tilting back as his eyes sought the ceiling. In spite of the warmth from the bottle he could not help shivering.

The door opened and Carol slipped back in, wearing her housecoat, carrying her toilet things, a bundle of her clothes and the lamp.

'Enter Florence Nightingale,' she said. 'Exit Prince Charming.'

He grinned, picked up his sponge-bag and towel, took the lamp from Carol and left. He met no one on his way to the bathroom. Inside, he set the lamp on the brown wooden case of the toilet cistern, poured water into the wash-hand basin. It was icy cold. Cleanliness, he told himself grimly, is next to godliness. In the mirror above the basin his face, lamplit, looked out at him from a backdrop of darkness. He began to undress.

When he got back to the bedroom he found Carol snuggled down under the bedclothes, only her head visible. Her hair seemed almost black against the pillowslip.

'I've been moving the bottles all over the bed like steam irons. It's not too bad now.' Out of the bedclothes came a slim, rounded arm. Her forefinger beckoned him. 'Come to bed, Mr Wilson.'

'I am coming.' He began to remove the sweater and trousers he had put on again in the bathroom after ablutions. The cold air wafted by his naked body as he strode to the bed, pulled back the clothes at his side to get his pyjamas. He halted. Carol lay on her side, facing him. She wore not the long sensible nightgown of the previous night but a light blue shortie nightie. Her gleaming shoulders reflected the mellow lamplight. The filmy blue material looked no more substantial than cobwebs.

He took a deep breath, swallowed. A dimple came and went in her cheeks as she looked at him. Her gaze dropped.

'Well, don't just stand there. Do something, if only to stop the heat getting out of this bed.'

He was in the bed and she was in his arms and they were wrapped in warmth though the room lay cold about them. And except for the gleam of lamplight in their eyes and its soft illumination of their faces, they gave themselves over to other senses, to touch and taste and intimate murmured endearments. Quietly the room listened to their loving requests and appreciations of joys shared and discoveries made. To him she was soft and smooth and warm, deliciously and secretly scented: to her he was strong and firm, hard and protective, demanding and gentle. And luck was with them. Their bodies gathered momentum together. The woman was ready when the man, driven by his urgent need, loomed above her. Her cry of amazement and joy when she received him was made to his own searching mouth.

Twice more that night they sought each other in the act of love. Between times she lay in his arms, their breaths mingling, their eyes scanning each other's face in the lamplight, their bodies warm together. Finally he got out of bed, put on his pyjamas, switched out one lamp and dimmed the other. Back beside her, he found her snuggled round with her back towards him.

'Good night,' he said, conscious of the word's inadequacy.

'Good night,' she murmured. 'Beats a hot-water bottle any time.'

He patted the soft, warm cheek of her hip under the thin nightie, marvelled at his lack of desire – a spent force, Wilson – turned round and within minutes was asleep.

He was awake, catapulted into instant alertness. He lay flat on his back, the ceiling dim above him. Beside him Carol slept on. For a minute he lay and listened. Was it the same as last night? Or were some of the others up there, in spite of their agreement not to set up a watching rota? He lay, straining his ears. It sounded just like the previous night, the tramp of a heavy man, measuring out the distance across the floor of the upstairs room. Again he noticed how cold the room was, how vapour condensed from his exhaled breath had dampened the sheet about his mouth.

He contrived to read the time on his watch. Ten past three. Later tonight. Or perhaps he had slept throughout most of it. A momentary warmth invaded him when he remembered that the earlier part of the night had not been uneventful, that sleep had been late in coming. And then the footsteps broke into his fond recollections.

He swung himself out of bed. Forgetting his dressing-gown, he put on socks and drew trousers and sweater over his pyjamas. Finding his slippers he padded to the window, pulled aside the heavy curtain. Tonight there were starlit patches amid broken clouds. But no other illumination. Blackness lay about the house, rendering the snow-covered countryside invisible.

A rumbling, scraping sound – the trunk dragged across a wooden floor noise – came from above. He dropped the curtain, crossed to the bedside table, retrieved the big rubber-covered torch. After checking his memory of the bedrooms' occupants from the chart, he opened the door. The hall was a black well.

Pollard and Hunt were in bedroom five, in the opposite corner of the floor; Meredith and Smith in bedroom four. Paul, his way illuminated by the cone of torchlight, walked round the gallery. He tapped on the doors of bedrooms four and five in succession and waited, shivering with excitement.

Both bedroom doors opened in quick succession. Pollard and Smith appeared. Paul's tension lessened slightly.

'The noises have started again. Footsteps and the dragging noise.'

'Right.' In the low illumination, Pollard's face was alert. Smith, yawning, was not as eager. Behind them Paul saw Hunt and Meredith.

'Give us a second to get something on,' said Pollard.

They disappeared, leaving the doors ajar. Paul remained on the dark, icy gallery, his tension rebuilding itself. Supposing the noises had stopped by the time they got upstairs to the room. He'd look a proper idiot. A dismaying thought struck him. Supposing they were still going on, but only he could hear them. He thought of Carol lying asleep in their bed and hoped she wouldn't wake up. She hadn't the previous night. Did that mean it was true? That only he could hear the noises . . .

The four men joined him, equipped with torches. Hunt also carried a battery-operated tape-recorder. Pollard seemed to have assumed command.

'Meredith, you and I will go up the stairs on this side, make our way along the servants' corridor. Jeremy, you and Ted and Wilson will go up the other flight. We'll meet outside the tower-room door.'

Paul found himself padding along the corridor to the foot of the narrow flight he had already climbed twice in the past twenty-four hours. The three men halted at the dark passageway with its bare, narrow steps leading upwards and listened. Paul could hear Hunt's open-mouthed breathing beside him. And something else. From somewhere upstairs, faintly but quite definitely, sounds came. He swallowed dryly. Could the others not . . . ?

'Ha!' The sergeant's breath was released. 'I hear it. Come on!'

They followed him as quietly as they could up the steep stairs. The sounds became clearer. Scraping sounds. At the top they saw the torches of the other men cascading light along the low passageway. In a pool of light cast by a single torch the five men listened. A rasping, scrabbling sound came from the end of the short corridor leading to the door of the tower-room.

'Hunt!' Meredith's whisper was urgent. 'Get the recorder on.'

'Yes. Oh yes!' The television producer's fingers fumbled at the buttons, lit from the torch held by Smith. The green magic eye blazed and the cassette spools began to turn. For two minutes that seemed as long as hours the men stood rigid as more noises, gasps, raps, throbbing sounds insinuated themselves on their hearing.

'All right,' said Meredith tensely. 'Let's go in. Hunt, keep the recorder running.'

The narrow passage seemed to crowd in upon them as they approached the door; the darkness seemed intent on suffocating their torch beams. Pollard, in the lead, turned the handle and pushed open the door.

They stepped into the seven-sided room, shone torches over walls, floor and ceiling, opened cupboards, examined the red seals on the uncurtained windows. The seals were intact. The room was empty, cold and morbidly depressing.

They stood round the octagonal table looking at each other, searching their torch-illumined faces for guidance.

'We did hear those noises from here,' said Hunt. 'Didn't we?'

Pollard nodded.

'We did. We all heard them. So at least we know that Wilson's story is . . . no story.'

Meredith moved.

'Hunt, play back the tape. Just to make sure.'

Startled, Hunt pressed the necessary buttons. And again the eerily irrelevant noises filled the room. At least, Paul thought, it was objective. His eyes narrowed. It was different somehow. Concentrating, he listened. Something was added. The hair bristled at the nape of his neck and the bitter cold of the room was suddenly even more sapping of his body heat.

'Turn it off!' he gasped. 'Listen!'

The recorder snapped silent. But something else remained, faint, elusive, so difficult to hear that he had to listen in total concentration. The others heard it too, the quiet, subdued lost sound of a woman weeping.

'For God's sake,' Smith muttered.

'It's not in this room,' Pollard stated. Meredith turned and faced the black chasm of the open door.

'No, it's down the stairs. Or along the passageway.'.

The distant sobs continued, declaring utter misery and hopelessness.

'All right.' Meredith's voice was too steady. 'We'd better get downstairs in any case. If we can hear this up here, it's probably very loud downstairs. I suggest we retrace our steps, meet on the first-floor gallery. Hunt, turn that recorder on again.'

They left the room to itself, found their way down the narrow, steep flight of steps. They met the others on the gallery. So far no one else seemed to have been wakened by the low sobbing, still audible, still nerve-scraping in its wretched loneliness.

And now it seemed to come from the dark vault of the hall

beneath them. It was insistent; it called on its listeners' stores of
pity and humanity, it tugged at each man's natural desire to help a
fellow being in distress.

They shone their torches down the stairs, followed the beams
down to the hall below. Speechlessly they crossed to the lounge
door, where a lingering trace of warmth still met them. They
entered the lounge, still led by the sounds. In the torchlight the
room appeared just as they had left it several hours before.

'I'll light the lamps,' said Pollard quietly. The click of his cigarette lighter sounded inordinately loud over the background of
sobs. The lamplight flooded the room after he replaced the cylindrical glass cover.

With a thrill of horror, Paul realized that the sounds now came
from beyond the nailed doors leading to the billiards-room. He
looked at Meredith. The man's fleshy face was starkly grim, his
mouth set. Hunt clutched the tape-recorder, his eyes wide, face
white. Smith's mouth was stretched in a rictus of fear. His eyes
showed outrage at his inability to comprehend what he heard.

Pollard walked to the doors, listened, his head bent. The sobs
were quieter, muffled by the closed doors, gasping as if an effort
at control was being made.

'If a couple of us went outside we might see something if we
shone torches through the window of the billiards-room.'

'I doubt it,' said Meredith.

Paul felt confused, sympathetic to Pollard's suggestion, but
cringing within at the thought of going out of the house into the
freezing cold of the night. Or, he thought, was he scared by the
possibility of actually seeing something inside the dark billiards-
room? He shivered.

'But surely we must have a look?' he heard himself saying.
'Surely we must try to . . .'

'Help?' Meredith's mouth grimaced. 'I appreciate your concern, Wilson. In God's truth, whatever is making those sounds
requires help. But I doubt if we're capable of giving it.'

Smith, legs apart, fists clenched, stared at the doors.

'Who do you think? What do you think it is?'

'I don't know.'

The tape-recorder shook in Hunt's hand.

'But who is it? Is it anything to do with Mary Rolfe? Or Mrs Howard?'

Meredith shrugged.

'It's possible.'

Pollard waved an arm.

'It's quieter now. Listen.'

The sobs were dying away. They were interrupted by longer and longer silences as if composure was gradually returning. Finally all was quiet beyond the barricaded doors.

As the five men stood there, frozen by the chill breath of their speculations, Paul thought of the evening's session with Ann Parish. The regression to Mary Rolfe seemed to have occurred ages ago. Was the unhappiness and death by drowning of the Victorian girl connected with the heart-broken weeping they had just heard? Or did it connect with the murder or suicide of Eleanor Howard? He did not know. All he knew was that he hated and loathed this house.

Meredith sighed.

'I think that's it for tonight. I suggest we get back to bed and try to get some sleep for the rest of the night. Of course, if anything else happens we'd better wake each other.'

Pollard nodded. While he extinguished the oil-lamps, Hunt switched off the recorder. Paul, shivering with cold, thought of Carol lying asleep upstairs. A vision of their love-making surfaced in healthy contrast to the miasma of wretchedness, fear and long-dead crimes that clung to the musty decaying walls of the fabric. He followed Smith from the lounge, knowing that all he desired in the world at that moment was to snuggle under the blankets behind Carol. Behind him Pollard, last man from the lounge, cast his torch beam over the dark interior, listened for a moment. Whoever you are, God help you, he thought bleakly. He turned and began to cross the hall after the others.

11   The Intruder

Carol woke, not fully, but to a dim awareness that she was no longer asleep. She was conscious enough to know she lay on her side, her knees bent. The room was quiet; the dimmed oil-lamp faintly illuminated the furniture. Through half-closed eyes she saw the dark bulk of the huge, old-fashioned wardrobe to the left of the closed door. She had the same feeling she sometimes experienced when she woke after a particularly pleasant dream, a warm, comfortable emotional tone. Then she recollected the earlier events of the night. Her lips parted and she sighed, snuggling down still farther in the warm blankets.

Vaguely she wondered what had awakened her. She was conscious of Paul's presence behind her. He shifted in the bed so that it creaked and she felt a gentle touch on her hip. His hand was cold through the thin fabric of her nightie. He must have been up to make his hand so cold. It moved down her flank in a stroking motion to the hem of the shortie nightwear on to the warm flesh of her upper thigh. She gasped. If he wanted to persuade her to co-operate with him again she was not unwilling to allow herself to be fully awakened. But he could wait until he had heated up. It was no fun having a hand like an ice block slipping under her nightie.

'Darling,' she breathed. 'If every bit of you is as cold as your hand, please wait a little.'

His touch stroked higher, up to her waist and began to move round to her stomach. She gasped once more as her flesh shrank inwards. Her voice sharpened.

'No, Paul, please. Wait.'

The touch tightened, the bed creaked again behind her and the first awakening of her pleasure was dispelled by annoyance at his heedless continuation. She was about to bring her own hand down to try to remove his icily exploring one when her eyes, open and fixed on the door, widened sharply. It was moving slowly inwards.

Fear flooded her mind. She jerked backwards against the heavier bulk behind her. Almost unconscious of the cold hand pressing and probing her body – or the chill spreading over her back and hips – she tried to wrench her eyes away from the opening door.

'Paul,' she whispered. 'The door. Look!'

She attempted to turn her head, tried to force her body round. In his need he seemed intent only in imprisoning her in his clasp. Her inability to move and the threat of what lay behind the opening door fired panic within her.

'No!' she gasped. 'No, no!'

Vaguely aware of a sound like exhaled breath in her ear, she saw a dim figure slip round the edge of the door. In the moment in which she recognized it her mind, wildly attempting to integrate perception before and around and behind her, crashed into uncomprehending, outraged panic.

Paul, just inside the door, froze motionless as her first shrieks tore the chill air of the room. He had hoped to slip into bed without awakening her. And she had thought he was an intruder. The sight of her convulsively flailing limbs under the heaving blankets and the continuing screams brought him to action. Striding to the bedside, he stooped towards her struggling body.

'It's all right, darling! It's me. You're safe. Calm down. It's me, darling. I've got you safe.' On and on he murmured his reassurances while he fought to contain her frenzied attempts at escape. Only when he was sitting on the edge of the bed, with the girl in his arms, her body twisted into his like that of a terrified child, did she begin to respond. By the time the others had arrived, she had controlled her shrieks of pure horror. Sobbing convulsively, her body trembling violently, her hands clutching painfully at him, she had recovered from the mindless state of terror sufficiently to recognize that this time she was in the arms of her husband.

They searched the room. Meredith and Pollard examined the window seals; Smith and Hunt opened the wardrobe, looked under the bed. Every space where someone could lie concealed was looked at. Carol, in housecoat now, standing before Paul with his arms about her, watched numbly. Occasionally a shivering fit seized her body. Bourne, wakened by her screams, stood just inside the door. Ann and Joyce, Cliff Swanson and Harry Fletcher clustered together on the gallery just beyond the open door.

The men found nothing. The telltale seals were intact.

Bourne, in a plum-coloured dressing-gown, thrust his hands into its cord-edged pockets.

'Mrs Wilson, I'm not quite sure I understand what happened. You say someone was in your bed. Mr Wilson, you were up?'

'Yes. Meredith, Hunt, Pollard, Smith and I were up. We had been downstairs and were coming back to our rooms when . . . when it happened.' He felt her tremble and tightened his grip about her.

'I see. Why were you up? Oh well, that doesn't matter at the moment. Mrs Wilson. You think there was someone in your bed.' The slightly drawn-out words proclaimed his scepticism.

'I know there was. Someone . . . or something.' Carol's voice was steady, but it was a steadiness fragile in extent. 'I felt a touch – it was icy! – I thought Paul had been up – had just come back – I . . . I was' – she swallowed – 'held tightly so that I couldn't move. I couldn't turn. And then when I saw Paul enter the room I knew I was being held by . . . something . . .'

'Quite so. You saw nothing?'

'It was behind me.' Her voice was almost hushed with horror. 'It kept behind me . . . holding me. When it pressed against me it felt like ice. I heard a sort of gasping-out-of-air sound. And when Paul appeared I managed one glance round before – before – well, before I started screaming.'

'And saw – ?'

'I don't know. There was a gap in the bedclothes.'

'A gap?'

'A sort of hollow with the clothes heaped above it. It was black and deep – ' Abruptly she shuddered.

'A hollow? What do you mean?'

'I don't know!' She shook her head violently. 'It was like a black pit with something in it. Something horrible. There was some-thing. I know that. And it knew what it was doing.'

'Knew what it was doing?' Bourne raised an eyebrow.

'It had' – she hesitated – 'purpose. It – it – oh God! *It stroked me!*'

With the slightest uplifting of a shoulder Bourne dismissed the whole episode.

'Now, Mrs Wilson,' he said urbanely, 'you must keep things in perspective. No one was found in the room. We've searched it thoroughly. Your husband has stated he saw nothing and that no one could have passed out of the room while he was here. Now it is possible that you were startled out of a deep sleep by your husband's arrival, or you had a nightmare brought on by the unusual circumstances of the house and its history – '

'That's not true! I was not asleep. I was awake. I know I was not alone in that bed. It held me – '

'Oh, but it's surely possible the bedclothes themselves were tucked in so tightly they seemed to hamper and cling to you – '

'No!' Tears sprang to her eyes, her head turned towards her husband. 'There was something, Paul. I swear it. Something vile!' Her voice rose dangerously high.

'Mrs Wilson.' Bourne's tones were the tones of an adult reasoning with a child. 'You really should – '

'Bourne, be quiet! Not another word,' Meredith cut in decisively, so curtly that the other man was left open-mouthed. 'Before you go on I insist that you listen to the tape that Hunt made.'

'Tape? What tape?'

Meredith glanced round the company before looking at his watch.

'Twenty-five past four. May I suggest that we all try to get some rest before morning. Let us try to have breakfast at nine. Afterwards we will meet in the lounge.' His face grave, he continued: 'I feel we should then try to think of some means of getting out of here.'

'I'm not sure that's possible,' said Pollard.

'Nevertheless I feel we ought to re-examine the possibilities carefully. Even to take some risk may be preferable to staying on here.'

'Rubbish!' Bourne's voice was almost petulant. 'You are being quite needlessly alarmist. Quite irresponsibly so. I intend to continue the programme of experiments we agreed on.'

Paul thought Meredith looked exhausted. The older man shrugged.

'Very well. You must do as you see fit. But we will discuss the matter again after breakfast.' He paused. 'After we have all heard that tape. And at the risk of being called a scaremonger, may I suggest that whenever possible we keep in pairs.'

With a snort of contempt Bourne turned on his heel and strode from the room. The others followed but more thought-fully. Meredith, his eyes troubled, turned to Paul and Carol.

'Try to get some rest. Why not refill those hot-water bottles.' He smiled briefly. 'See you in the morning.'

After he'd gone, Paul dug the bottles out of the disturbed bed.

'You carry the oil-lamp,' he suggested.

She nodded. He knew nothing could have kept her from accompanying him downstairs.

In the old kitchen, while the kettles boiled on the bright hiss-ing calor gas flames, he stood as he had stood in the bedroom with his arms round her, both of them facing the stove. Neither spoke until the kettle lids began to rattle under the steam pres-sure. As he moved to empty the bottles she said:

'Paul, I wasn't asleep. I didn't dream it.'

He looked at her, at the wide blue eyes shadowed beneath by shock. Holding the kettle handle by means of a dish-towel he began to pour the water into the first bottle. What do I say? he thought. If I say I believe her she'll take it that indeed there was something ghastly in that bed. If I pooh-pooh the idea – like that bastard Bourne – she'll feel I believe she was stupidly hys-terical.

'Darling, I believe you. But what it means I simply do not know.'

'What was that tape Meredith mentioned?'

'Some sounds we heard. That's why I was up in the first place.'

'Sounds?'

'Yes. You'll hear them in the morning.' He began to fill the second bottle. She took in a deep breath.

'The morning can't come too soon. Paul, promise me you won't leave me alone. If I wake again in that damned room and find you gone – '

'Don't worry, darling. I'll stick close to you.'

'Promise.' She smiled tremulously. 'Even if you hear a regiment marching by. Promise me you won't leave me alone. At any time.'

'I promise.' He tried to inject a lighter note. 'If you insist I'll even accompany you to the bathroom.'

'It may come to that,' she breathed. 'Modesty is the least of my worries.'

He picked up the bottles.

'Come on, darling. Light the way to bed.'

They lay together, her back curled against his front, his right arm under her neck, his right hand clasping her upturned left hand. He stretched his left arm and hand across her warm upper thigh. At their feet the hot bottles radiated their heat throughout the bed. But her solar plexus was rigid with fear even as his mouth was dry with uncertainty.

'Go to sleep, darling,' he whispered. 'I'm here.'

Even after he was sure she had finally dropped off, he lay awake, uneasy thoughts and speculations coursing obsessively through the tired labyrinths of his mind. Sleep did not come during the rest of that night; at best he achieved a dazed tense doze through which there ran the barbed wire of his anxiety.

12   Confession

They gathered in the lounge after breakfast. The fire burned high and hotly: daylight was brighter this morning but it looked just as cold outside with no sign of a thaw disturbing the thick white drifts covering the bleak landscape.

Bourne, a non-committal expression on his face, watched while Hunt set the portable tape-recorder on the occasional table lifted forward to the centre of the semicircle of chairs and couches. In a few, almost abrupt, sentences Meredith described the circumstances in which the recording had been made. Finally he nodded.

'All right, Mr Hunt.'

Paul, seated beside Carol, found his attention caught by the faces of the other occupants of the room. While the scraping noises, the footsteps and dragging, rumbling sounds were being replayed, the others sat quite motionless, faces solemn and grave with concentration. Occasionally their eyes would search other faces as if seeking to learn what their companions thought of it. But when the weeping began, its harrowing effect seemed to sear into the composure of the listeners. Ann Parish went chalk-white; Joyce Mair, her face taut with fear, bit the side of her forefinger. Paul thought he heard Smith swear softly under his breath and he saw Hunt tug at his curly black beard. Bourne listened, his mouth set. Occasionally he raised his head, his eyes unseeing in his effort to assess the meaning behind the heart-rending sobs.

Finally it was over. Hunt switched off, returned to his seat. Joyce Mair, looking utterly stricken, gazed at the battened double doors leading to the billiards-room. Her voice was almost a whisper.

'What is it?'

Meredith, with bitter irony, turned to Bourne.

'Would you care to enlighten her?'

Bourne, for once seemingly at a loss for words, hesitated. Pollard scratched his chin.

'Somehow it seems almost worse in daylight. Meredith, do you think . . . ?' He hesitated.

'Yes?'

'Do you think it possible the sounds and the sobbing were meant to, well, to distract our attention?'

'That would imply purpose.'

'Yes.'

'Well, I don't know about that. The phenomena may be no more than the rerunning of past events in this house.'

Jeremy Hunt looked puzzled. 'But if that is so, how could it be dangerous?'

'If it is so it would not be dangerous. But we don't know that for sure.' Carol saw him look at her then look away quickly as if regretting she had caught him doing so. She felt again that cold leaden touch at her stomach. Did Pollard and Meredith think it possible Paul had been lured from their bed so that that thing . . . ? She shivered.

Ann Parish turned to Bourne. 'Dr Bourne, what do you think? Do you think we are in any real danger here?'

'None whatsoever!'

'The tape –'

'The tape is interesting. Very interesting indeed. I am even prepared to admit that so far I see no explanation in normal terms. But danger? Nonsense. There is no danger here beyond letting our nerves and imagination get the better of us. I see no reason why we shouldn't continue our experiments. Jeremy, I take it that meets with your approval?'

'What? Er – yes. Of course. Cliff? Joyce? Harry? Okay?'

In their own ways they signified their agreement. Harry's laugh was without much humour.

'It looks as if we're stuck here anyway so why not.'

By ten a.m. the camera and lights had been set up and Ann had been once more returned to the morning of the day on which Mary Rolfe died. In complete silence the onlookers listened and watched as Bourne began again his conversation with the entity claiming to be Mary Rolfe.

'Mary, you've told me you are worried about something, that it's making you very unhappy. Isn't that so?'

'Yes.'

'But you know now you can tell me about it.'

'I don't know.'

'But we talked about this. You remember I am one of your dream people?'

'Yes.'

'Then you know that you can talk to me about it. If I am one of your dream people it will remain a secret, won't it?'

'I suppose so.' Doubtfully.

'Of course it will.'

Paul found himself frowning at the strangeness of the situation.

Mary Rolfe was dead. She had died almost a century ago. She had left this house one summer afternoon near the end of the Victorian era and had drowned – or been drowned – in the sea-loch. This personification claiming to be Mary Rolfe could not exist. And yet here was Dr Arnold Bourne, alive and well and living in the late twentieth century, pretending to be a figment of 'Mary Rolfe's' imagination in order to persuade her to confide in him. Was it really possible that in the girl asleep on the couch they had a window into the nineteenth century, that the dead past could be resurrected and contacted?

'Now why are you unhappy, Mary?' Bourne's voice was warm and sympathetic. The bastard would have made a good psychiatrist, Paul thought.

'He's gone off me.'

'Who has?'

'He says he hasn't. He says we have to wait longer but I know he's gone off me.'

'Mary, you can tell me. Who are you speaking of?'

'Arthur.' The voice was a whisper. Startled, the listeners looked at each other in conjecture.

'You mean . . .' Bourne hesitated, frowning '. . . Arthur Howard?'

'Yes.' The word was accompanied by a deep sigh.

'You believe Arthur Howard was – is – fond of you?'

'He loved me. He still says he does.'

Bourne, his face blank, wrinkled his brows, uncertain how to proceed.

'Mary, when did you first discover that Arthur Howard loved you?'

'It was August. I saw him looking at me. I knew he was interested in me. A girl can always tell. We met several times. In the grounds. Up the glen in the mountains.' A reminiscent half-smile appeared on the face that was Ann Parish's and in some strange way was not. 'He told me how unhappy he was, how he'd never really known what it was to be happy until he was with me. He said how much he needed me.'

Paul thought: that is exactly the way it would have happened if it is true. That is the way Howard would have operated. For it's the way it did happen generation after generation, even down to our sophisticated seventies.

Now that her reluctance to talk had been overcome, Mary Rolfe required little prompting to relate how the affair had proceeded. Clandestine meetings outside the house, visits to her room – as Mrs Howard's personal maid, she had a servant's room to herself – it was clear that Mary had gone at least halfway to meet Howard.

'Did Mrs Howard not suspect?' Bourne asked.

'No.' The negative was drawn out scornfully. 'She was too busy with her headaches, and moans about her lost babies and how dreary and lonely it was up here. No. She didn't know.

'I don't suppose she'd really have cared much if she had known. That's what made it so unfair.'

'Unfair?'

'Yes. We loved each other and wanted to be together all the time and yet Arthur couldn't do anything about it. He said the scandal of a divorce would ruin him. Anyway she'd have to divorce him and she wouldn't do that.' In vitriolic tones. 'She believed all that stuff about marriage being for keeps.'

'You must have been worried when Mr Howard was arrested for murder.'

'I was an' all. I nearly went off my head.'

'Do you think he did it?'

'Did what?'

'Killed his wife.'

'Killed her.' With eyes still shut, the body of Ann Parish rocked with laughter, a bitter humourless outburst all the more shocking because of its unexpectedness. 'Of course he didn't kill her. I killed her. I was the one who poisoned her.'

13   The Labyrinths of Time

In their own ways the listeners reacted. Bourne recovered quickly.

'Why did you poison her?'

'It's obvious, isn't it? While she was alive Arthur was married to her. He could only be free to marry me if she died. We loved each other. What was the good of three people being miserable when two could be happy?'

'How did you manage it, Mary?'

'Oh, it wasn't difficult. Arthur showed me his collection of poisons, one day when we were alone in the house. He even explained what they did. So I knew which one to use. I decided to slip it into her water bottle. She always took one tumbler full of cold water last thing at night. Later I went into the bedroom and took away the bottle. I cleaned it out, refilled it.'

Surely, Paul told himself, it was role-taking on Ann Parish's part. Surely it was the way hypnotized subjects had of acting the part, plausibly and with a wealth of circumstantial detail. And yet it was difficult not to be persuaded that this was Mary Elizabeth Rolfe describing how she had murdered Eleanor Howard in eighteen-ninety-one.

'How did you get the poison, Mary?'

'I've told you.' The slightly hard voice registered surprise. 'From Arthur's collection.'

'I know that. But didn't he keep it under lock and key?'

' 'Course he did. But every night he emptied his pockets and put his money and keys and things on the dressing-table in his bedroom. I managed to borrow the keys early one morning before they were up. I used to take morning tea up to them.'

'Does he know you killed his wife?'

'I told him not long before they arrested him. I said that if he was arrested I would immediately confess so that he could be set free.'

'And why didn't you?'

'He wouldn't hear of it.' There was pride in her voice. 'He said he'd stand trial and save me.'

I'll bet, thought Paul. Howard knew that if she confessed at the very least he'd probably get a heavy prison sentence as accessory before the deed. It was all too obvious that even if he had not asked her explicitly to poison his wife he had planted the idea firmly in her head by dangling marriage before her, showing her the poisons and explaining which ones were the most suitable. So he had nothing to lose by standing trial. No wonder he appeared confident. He knew that if he were found guilty the love-crazed girl would own up in time and he would be saved.

'But how could you have convinced the authorities that you had killed Mrs Howard?'

'I kept the poison bottle.'

'Why did you do that?'

'At first I thought I'd leave it beside the water bottle so that they'd think she had emptied it. Then I thought he might be blamed. So I kept it.'

'What did you do with it?'

'I hid it. In a safe place.'

'Where did you hide it, Mary?'

'In my bedroom. There's a loose floorboard. I put it under it.'

'I see. I suppose you got rid of it after the trial?'

'No.'

'You mean it was – it is still there?'

'Yes.'

To Paul it seemed that all the listeners caught the extraordinary implications of this statement at the same time. According to the records this was the last day of Mary Rolfe's life. If she was telling the truth – Paul shook himself mentally – that is if this entity claiming to be Mary Rolfe was actually giving them the truth, then when Mary Rolfe died, the poison bottle was still concealed under the floorboard.

'Does Mr Howard know you still have the bottle?'

'No. I just said I'd confess if he was found guilty.'

'Which bedroom did – do you have?'

'One upstairs. On the servants' floor.'

'Is it the one next to the tower-room?'

'No. It's the next one.'

'The middle one.'

'Yes.'

'Where is the floorboard?'

'Under the bed.'

'When you've just entered the room is it to the left of the window?'

'Yes.'

'Is it near the left-hand wall?'

'Yes.'

'Good. Now, Mary, I want you to rest for a while. Rest.'

Bourne straightened up and looked at the others.

'Discussion?' he suggested. Meredith nodded.

'Then I'll bring her out of it.'

And as before he brought Ann Parish back to herself and wakened her. A minute or so later, she and Carol left the lounge to begin preparations for lunch.

They looked at each other for a moment. Hunt was patently pleased by the turn of events.

'You're going to search, aren't you?'

'Of course.' Meredith blinked behind his glasses. 'This was the sort of thing we hoped for when we planned this visit. At least – we didn't quite know what to expect. We certainly did not expect a poison bottle could have lain undisturbed to the present day. Yes, we'll search.'

'But you don't really think that bottle's still there, do you?' Paul's mind shrank from the implications.

'Why not?' Bourne replied. 'If it happened as it has been told to us, then Mary Rolfe could not have removed it for she died that afternoon.'

'Not unless,' Pollard said slowly, 'she remembered her conversation with you, Dr Bourne, later that morning and removed it before she went out boating with William Metcalfe.'

There was dead silence. Bourne looked blankly at Pollard.

'Oh come now – ' Then he stopped, his eyes narrowing. 'If I get your train of thought, Captain Pollard, you're speculating on the possibility that by talking with the entity claiming to be Mary Rolfe we are in some way actually putting thoughts into the mind of Mary Rolfe living in the late nineteenth century?'

Pollard shrugged. 'I know it sounds totally against common sense but is it?'

'What you're saying,' said Meredith, 'is that although Mary Rolfe in common-sense parlance lived in the late nineteenth century, and we are living in the late twentieth, Ann Parish as Mary Rolfe could actually be living simultaneously in eighteen-ninety-two.'

'Something like that. She remembered you, Dr Bourne, talking to her. You remember when you asked her what day it was she said: "I've told you that before"? Now, did that memory register in Ann Parish's brain or did it in some way become part of Mary Rolfe's memory store as well? If that is so, perhaps your concern about the bottle will cause her' – he grinned – 'we need new tenses for this, don't we? – will make her get rid of it, before she goes boating this afternoon.'

Bourne sighed.

'Ingenious, and intriguing, but quite without foundation, I'm afraid. One can quite easily dismiss it.'

'How?'

'Because if it were true, we could change the past. Suppose for the sake of argument I convince Mary Rolfe that she will be drowned by William if she goes out in the boat with him this afternoon. She does not go and therefore survives, perhaps to live another forty years. Suppose she marries and has children, one of them becoming a doctor who discovers penicillin ten years before Alexander Fleming. Then most of the thousands who died in the thirties from septicaemia would have lived. And so on. No. It would become a snowball rolling down the slope of time altering history in ever-growing measure with each passing second. It cannot be true. We know Mary Rolfe drowned in eighteen-ninety-two. Nothing can alter that.'

'But,' queried Meredith, 'would we know?'

'What do you mean?'

'Surely it also follows that if as a consequence of Mary Rolfe's survival men and women are born and live – and other men and women are never born because their potential fathers and mothers never met, having married Mary Rolfe's descendants instead – surely it also follows that all other threads in the fabric of history are unpicked and rewoven, such as the newspaper records *and our memories of having read these records?*' Meredith shook his head slowly. 'No, Bourne, you can't dismiss the possibility that way.'

'I wish I'd never thought of it,' said Pollard ruefully. 'I'm getting a giddy vision of history shuffling and reshuffling itself endlessly like a restless sea.'

'All right,' said Bourne. 'I take the point. It could be but if so it's unverifiable. But that still leaves the poison bottle. Suppose we find it upstairs?'

'If we do,' Paul said, 'I don't see how it's possible to avoid the conclusion that in some way Ann Parish was Mary Rolfe in a former life.'

'The reincarnation hypothesis?' Hunt asked.

He broke off, dabbing at his trousers-leg. On the thigh a black spot had appeared. As he did so a second damp spot stained the cloth. He looked up in time to see several drops of a clear fluid fall from the ceiling.

Paul looked upwards. Startled he saw a steady sequence of drips form and fall from the ceiling. Even as he watched, more points of the ceiling began to leak. Gasps and exclamations came from Meredith and Bourne as they felt drops fall on them. In a state of bemusement they watched the liquid rain down.

'It must be a burst pipe!' said Pollard. Meredith drew out a handkerchief, rubbed his thigh.

'Pollard, will you and Smith go upstairs to the bedroom above us and see what you can see.'

'Right. Come on, Ted.'

When they'd left, the others continued to watch. A faint familiar odour came to their nostrils. Paul knelt and gingerly rubbed a finger in a small puddle near the fireplace. He sniffed the tip of his finger, very tentatively tasted it.

'It's whisky!'

Hunt followed his example.

'For God's sake! This is gin.'

The strange rain had stopped. The plaster of the ceiling was dry and quite unbroken. Only the damp patches and glistening pools on the floor remained to testify that it had ever happened. In an almost abstracted, totally uncertain way, Hunt ran his hands through his hair.

'This is – we must, ah, certainly we've got to get this on film. Harry!'

'No, wait a minute.' Meredith held up a hand. 'Mr Wilson, will you and Dr Bourne go to the dining-room and bring back the bottles of whisky and gin we brought.'

Paul looked at Bourne. Without a word they left the lounge. The dining-room was empty. From the kitchen the voices of Ann and Carol could be heard. The men crossed to the sideboard. Paul picked up the bottle of Grouse whisky and froze as he registered its weight.

'Empty.'

Bourne lifted the bottle of Gordon's gin.

'This is also empty.'

They returned to the lounge with the bottles. Meredith did not seem surprised.

'They were almost full last night when I poured our nightcap. You'll remember we emptied the previous bottles and just started on these.'

Cliff Swanson rubbed his chin. 'You really think this' – he indicated the liquid spilled on the floor – 'came from them?'

'I do. The only other explanation is that we have a secret drinker who emptied the bottles last night. But that still leaves this.' He pointed to the pools.

'But why?' Hunt almost yelled the question. Meredith frowned.

'No idea. And if you ask "how?" I can't answer that either.'

'But this is ridiculous,' Bourne snapped. 'It's a trick! It must be a trick of some sort.' He raised his head, glared around him. 'Well, I'll get to the bottom of it. I'll beat it yet!'

He whirled as Pollard and Smith re-entered the lounge. 'Well, did you find anything?'

'No. What about the water. Is it still coming in?'

Meredith showed Pollard and Smith the empty bottles. The two men tested the liquids for themselves.

'Extraordinary,' Pollard commented. Smith sniffed.

'The place smells like a brewery. What a waste. Do you think whatever it is is going to spoil all our booze this way?'

Paul thought Meredith's mask of concern was well beyond what one might have expected over the loss of a couple of bottles of whisky and gin, even in such bizarre circumstances. It was almost as if he was worried sick about something else, something he did not want to voice.

'I don't know,' he muttered. 'What I do know is that after lunch we should dig out the vehicles and stock them with fuel, food, blankets and some of our clothes.'

Pollard, whom he seemed to be addressing, narrowed his eyes.

'You speak as if you expect us to have to leave the house.'

Meredith drew in a deep breath.

'I don't know. But I think it could come to that.'

Bourne snorted.

'What absolute rubbish! Meredith, this scaremongering must

stop. It's – it's – ' He looked exasperatedly at him. 'What on earth could happen to drive us from the house? I suppose you'll be saying next we should leave now and huddle together in the cars.'

'No. I appreciate that common sense says we should remain where there's shelter, food and warmth. But at least let's have places we can go to, as a last resort.'

Pollard's grey eyes examined his face keenly.

'It's not bad sense, you know. I just don't see what could happen to drive us out of this place ... unless – ' He broke off, to glance thoughtfully at a small pool of whisky glinting on the floor. 'Unless – '

'Don't say it!' Meredith's voice was sharp. His eyes swept the faces of the occupants of the room. 'Believe me, I am speaking from experience. Do not voice any speculations that may occur to you about what could force us to leave this house. Don't even dwell on them too much in thought.'

'Oh, for heaven's sake,' said Hunt. 'You'll be saying next that walls have ears!' But his eyes worried round the room.

Bourne was at his most waspish.

'With all due respect, Meredith, you are behaving less like a parapsychologist than a maiden aunt. Perhaps you would like us to begin looking under our beds.'

Pollard ignored him. 'I agree with you, Meredith. At least let us get some food in the cars. And it might not be a bad idea to put blankets and clothes in them as well.' Something in his tone of voice and expression persuaded several of the others. They nodded. Paul saw Meredith exhale with relief.

'Good. After lunch we'll stock up the cars.' He turned to Bourne. 'And then I gather you'll want to check on Mary Rolfe's story of the poison bottle?'

Bourne nodded shortly, lines of dissatisfaction carved deep on his face from nose to mouth. As they rose for lunch, Paul saw that more snow had come with large flakes dropping like miniature parachutists on to already occupied territory.

14   One Secret Revealed

In the event Bourne had to possess his soul in patience while Pollard, Swanson, Paul and Fletcher dug out the vehicles once more prior to stocking them. It was a chilly, seemingly futile task with the falling snow promising to undo their efforts. Inside the house, Carol, Ann and Joyce began to fetch blankets from the linen cupboard on the first floor and stretch them out before the fires in the lounge and dining-room. Meanwhile Hunt and Meredith selected tins of meat and biscuits, coffee, jars of Bovril, some pans, a kettle, matches, a small calor-gas double-ring stove and a camping-gas container.

The outside door was finally locked and resealed. The camera and lights were carried upstairs, along the corridor and up the narrow steep servants' stairs to be set up within the middle attic room. The glare of light revealed in all its starkness the mean cramping sparseness of the room, its ancient peeling wallpaper, the cobwebs, the sloping ceiling. The room was empty apart from the lonely, forgotten rocking-horse in the corner, blindly facing the wall.

The camera was placed in one corner of the cold room, Fletcher behind it. Joyce went through the clapperboard ritual and stepped aside. Bourne watched while Pollard and Smith tried to roll back the worn, dun, patternless linoleum. It was so ancient it cracked and crumbled, frayed fragments breaking off to be thrown into a corner. Underneath they saw a dusty layer of old newspapers. The floorboards were filthy below the papers. Ann and Meredith stood by the door just inside the room, Hunt beside them. Carol and Paul stood behind them in the threshold.

'As far as we know,' said Bourne, 'the loose floorboard was somewhere near the middle, near the left-hand wall.'

Pollard and Smith tested the region, stamping with their feet on each board. None seemed loose. Pollard rubbed his chin, leaving a smear of dust on it.

'Well, there's nothing for it. We'll have to lift them one by one.'

'No, wait!' Bourne's eyes glinted. 'There's another way. Ann, would you please step forward.'

The young woman did so, obviously puzzled by the proceedings.

'Ann, I wonder if we may try hypnotizing you here?'

With only a moment's hesitation, she agreed.

'Good. Now this time although you will go under, you will remain standing. All right?'

'Yes.'

'Fine. Ten, five, nine, four, eight, three, seven, two, six, one. Sleep!'

The girl's head tilted forward, her eyes closed, her body seemed to relax but she remained upright. Over in the corner the eye and film of the camera saw and recorded as Bourne regressed the young woman to the year eighteen-ninety-two. And once again, for the last time, the voice of Mary Rolfe was heard.

'Now, Mary, you are in your bedroom.'

'Yes.' The tone was listless, uninterested.

'Come with me to the door.' Bourne waved the watchers backwards into the low passageway even as he took the girl by the arm. Slowly, like a somnambulist, she allowed herself to be steered to the threshold.

'Now, Mary, you are just entering your bedroom. You have the feeling that someone may have discovered the loose board. You are going to cross to it and check that the bottle is still there.'

For a moment she hesitated then moved forward, her eyes still closed. She stepped round something, crossed to the left-hand wall and knelt, left hand leaning against it. In doing so she made a gesture with the right that Paul realized with an icy shiver was the raising of a long skirt. Her right hand reached out – under her bed? – and felt across the boards. The watchers saw her fingers press the floor, feeling, testing. A frown of perplexity appeared on her face. Meredith felt his unease deepen.

'She's mixing up her eighteen-ninety-two memories with present-day sense data,' he whispered tensely.

The girl sobbed. She stood up, her back and hands pressed to the wall. Her eyes opened. Slowly her gaze roamed the room. Perplexity changed to horror.

'Who are you?' Her dark eyebrows arched upwards above wide open eyes. 'Where am I?' She swung her head towards the window. 'Snow! But it's summer.' In utter confusion she gasped, her breast heaving. 'I – Who – ? My room. Where is everything?' Her head tilted forward and bewilderment twisted her features as she took in the sweater and green trousers she wore. Her hands shot up to cover her face. 'I'm dead! I must be dead!' She raised her head, sparks in her eyes reflecting the lights. 'Is it Hell? Am I in Hell? I didn't mean to do it! I didn't! Oh please. Oh God! Oh God! Help me, help me!'

Racking sobs and cries escaped her. She sank to her knees, tears running down her cheeks.

It had all happened so quickly and dramatically that the onlookers remained spellbound. The first move was made by Meredith.

'Calm down, Mary, calm down my dear. Be quiet and listen. We are your friends. Calm down. Let me help you.' With a sharp gesture he stilled Bourne's angry and tentative movement. That it commanded Bourne at all was probably due to the neurologist's uncomprehending astonishment that Mary Rolfe had not only seen the others but was also listening and responding to the kindness and warmth in Meredith's voice. Still on her knees, she quietened bit by bit, her head raised towards Meredith, her shining eyes fixed on his face.

'Mary, my dear, what is the last thing you remember?'

'Please. I'm all confused. . . .' The girl's head swung wearily from side to side, her wet cheeks glistening.

'You've been confused a long time, haven't you?'

'Yes. A long time.'

'Tell me about it.'

'I don't seem to be well – at least I'm not myself. I can't talk to people, they don't listen. Somehow it's different here now. Lots of people I don't recognize. Sometimes I'm alone. I'm lost. And afraid. I'm so tired. Please, sir, where am I?'

'Mary, do you remember going out in a boat?'

The brows furrowed, the tear-filled eyes seemed to gaze into an immensity of space. The head moved slowly up and down.

'Y-yes.'

'What happened?'

'We sailed. It was a warm day.' The frown returned. 'William turned the boat over. I fell in the water. I couldn't swim . . . I'm sorry, sir, everything is sort of . . . funny after that. Mixed up.'

Meredith spoke very gently.

'Mary, if you fell into deep water, and couldn't swim, and William couldn't save you, what would happen?'

'I'd drown.' The eyes widened. 'I'd drown. Oh no! Did I drown? If I am dead where am I now. How can I be dead if I am speaking to you?'

'Mary, look at your hands, at your clothes. Are they yours?'

She raised her hands, turned them over, plucked at the fabric of the sweater. Beseechingly she looked at Meredith, the look of a hurt animal caught in a trap, hopeless, perplexed.

'Mary, you passed over. You drowned. A long time ago. The body you inhabit now belongs to another person. It is time now for you to go, my dear.'

'To go? Where can I go, sir? I've been wicked. I poisoned the mistress. I keep thinking about that. I can't get away from that.'

'That was a long time ago. You've been confused, Mary. You've been held here by your feelings. It is time for you to go on now.' Meredith swallowed. 'Look about you, Mary. With the inner eye. Close your eyes. What do you see?'

The eyelids dropped as if heavy with weariness.

'What do you see, Mary?'

'Some light. Far away.'

'Go towards it. Go now, my dear. Leave us and go towards that light. You will find friends there. Go.'

The body of Ann Parish swayed. Meredith signed to Bourne. The neurologist, though startled, read his cue correctly and began to bring Ann Parish out of the trance. She woke, blinked once or twice, looked enquiringly about. Surprise registered on her face as she realized she was on her knees. She got up, grimacing at the dust-patches on her trousers.

Meredith looked at her.

'How do you feel, Ann?'

'Fine. Was everything all right?'

'Yes. Everything was all right.' He turned to Bourne. 'We can discuss this downstairs later. But I will say one thing now. That must be the last session with Ann. You agree.'

Paul detected a note of steel in his voice. Bourne nodded slowly. Pollard pointed to the floor.

'Do we have that up now?'

Bourne nodded again.

Amid much creaking and rasping, Pollard and Smith managed to prise up the floorboard. A torch was shone into the cavity below, filled with the dust and cobwebs of the years.

Gritting his teeth, Pollard gingerly pushed his hand through the accumulated debris and began with care to dredge to the bottom of the foot-deep hole. The onlookers watched tensely. They saw him stiffen. Slowly he brought his hand out of the cavity. His fingers uncurled and his hand, palm up, was held out. On it there lay a small, cylindrical bottle, corkless, almost chalky with dust. With the forefinger of his other hand he smoothed away the dust layer. A label was uncovered. In copperplate handwriting, faint but still legible, were the words: *Tartar Emetic.*

15   Death-trap?

They returned to the lounge, leaving Swanson and Fletcher to bring down the camera and lighting equipment.

'Surely we'll get away soon,' Carol murmured. Paul drew her attention to the bay window where flurries of snow cascaded against the panes.

'I wouldn't count on it.' He turned to Pollard. 'There's not much use trying to get to the bridge today.'

'No. It's almost four-thirty. Daylight's going soon.'

Joyce shivered.

'So that means another night in this hole.' She hugged her knees, looked across at Meredith. 'Mr Meredith, can I ask you about what happened upstairs?'

'Yes,' Hunt added. 'You seemed to know what was going on.'

Bourne's eyes swung to Ann.

'Now we agreed not to discuss anything with Ann present.'

'I know,' Meredith resettled his glasses. 'But we also agreed that Ann would not be used again. So I see no point in not discussing what transpired upstairs. So, Ann, don't leave. You deserve to warm yourself by the fire. That room was like a vault upstairs.'

'Very well.' Bourne acquiesced with ill-grace. Ann smiled.

'You mean I actually get to know what happened upstairs?'

Meredith nodded.

'You appeared to slip from a hypnotic state into a trance state in which you were controlled by an entity claiming to be the spirit of Mary Elizabeth Rolfe, a maid in this house in the late nineteenth century.'

'So it wasn't the usual – what do you call it? – regression.'

Joyce looked at Ann. 'It's true. Mary Rolfe spoke through you to Mr Meredith. She said she had been confused for a long time. She didn't seem to know she was dead.'

'There is a famous book,' said Meredith, 'called *Thirty Years among the Dead* by Dr Karl Wickland. Dr Wickland was a psychiatrist. He believed that some of his most disturbed patients were possessed by the surviving entities of deceased persons – persons who had departed this life by suicide, by execution, under the most personality-damaging effects of drink or drugs. These entities were – to use a spiritualist term – earth-bound and occasionally were able to "enter" and in some respects take over certain living people whose minds happened to be in a receptive state.

'Now Dr Wickland claimed that when he gave shock treatment to such patients the invading entities disliked it so much that they temporarily left their victims.'

'But this is medieval superstition!' Bourne exploded. 'It's simply the old fantasy of believing mental illness was caused by demons and ill-treating the luckless sufferer to drive away the demon. Barbaric nonsense!'

Meredith nodded. 'Perhaps. Nevertheless, let me finish. Karl Wickland's wife had mediumistic powers. It appeared that once the entity had been driven from the patient, it slipped into the entranced body of Mrs Wickland, temporarily controlling her. There it could be questioned and reasoned with by Dr Wickland and the circle of friends who helped him in this rescue work.

'Let me summarize the common features of the case histories described in Wickland's book.

'The entity had not realized it was dead. Its death, as I've said, had been caused usually by violence, or was the result of drugs or drink. In its post-death state the entity had experienced a world composed of an irrational mixture of memories, obsessive desires, visions of people dead – and others still alive, a world of utterly confusing impressions.'

'Sounds like a dream-state,' Pollard commented.

'Exactly! Very like the dream in which we wander, confused and unable to recognize the most ludicrous inconsistencies, accepting but not analysing. But for these luckless entities a world also coloured by despair, regret, loneliness, longing, bitterness.' He sighed. 'It would appear, if we can accept Dr Wickland's theory, that at least some people survive death for a time but what survives exists obsessed with what it believed in while alive and no longer with access to the brain's analytical engine.'

'A pretty gloomy prospect,' Hunt murmured.

'Indeed it is. Anyway, Wickland found that while controlling his wife, the entity could be contacted, could be brought to recognize its situation and break free of its obsessions. You know, the overwhelming impression given by such cases is that the entity has so wrapped its own cloak of pseudoreality about it that it is oblivious to the attempts of other entities to help it. Until it recognizes its state, it is condemned to wander in its lonely twilight existence, creating its trail of havoc.'

'What was the outcome of such cases?' Ann asked.

'Invariably – sometimes after a very long struggle – the entity realized its situation, seemed to perceive a happier place to go to, and departed.'

'And you tried the Wickland technique upstairs with Mary Rolfe,' Pollard said.

'Yes. It seemed the reasonable thing to do. Whoever or whatever was the entity possessing Ann, whether or not it was the regression entity, it was begging for help. I hope to God we gave it.'

'The weeping we heard,' Paul said. 'Will that return?'

'Possibly not.'

'But surely, if what you've said is true, we can now accept that Mary Rolfe's shade will no longer trouble us at night.'

Meredith shook his head. 'I can't guarantee that. In fact I'd say we should remain as firmly on our guard as before.'

'You mean – ?' Paul broke off.

'I mean I believe there's something else here.'

Paul and Carol spoke together.

'The man I saw –'

'The thing in my bed –'

Meredith regarded them steadily.

'Whatever destroyed Bernard Gray. That may still be here.'

'What! After almost a century?' Hunt was openly scoffing.

'What is time?' Meredith asked. 'Karl Wickland's entities would appear to have been active for many decades and seemingly could have gone on indefinitely. No. I hope I'm wrong but in case I'm not, take care.'

Slashing across his last words came the most appalling crash, a noise as loud as if a forty-tonner juggernaut lorry had collided with a brick wall. The room shook, dust and plaster drifting from the ceiling. Shocked, they scrambled speechless to their feet.

Pollard leaped to the lounge door, threw it open and stopped. They crowded behind him. Outside, the hall floor and the staircase were almost hidden under heaps of snow, broken wood, jagged pieces of glass, twisted lead sheets. Freezing air bit at their lungs. And where the large domed skylight had been, a gap as wide as the hall lay open revealing a darkish opaque sky from which snow fell heavily and silently into the house.

To Paul's horror he saw an arm sticking up above the largest heap of snow and debris. Even as he watched, a red patch began to spread over the snow. A few treads above, another mound of debris covered a second body lying sprawled down the stairs.

The men clambered over the snow and fragments of the dome, began to work frantically. They got Fletcher uncovered first. He bled to death even as Bourne worked, his jugular severed by a razor-sharp shard of glass. Afterwards Bourne conjectured that he must have heard the preliminary creaking and splintering, tilted back his head and received the knife-like fragment in his throat.

Swanson was dead when they got him out. His neck was

broken, his skull crushed. With ashen faces, the men carried the bodies upstairs to the bedroom the dead men had occupied. Placing them on their beds, they drew sheets over them before leaving the room. They had crunched down the stairs again and were crossing the filthy, littered, slaughterhouse-like hall when they halted. All around them, softly but insistently, the air vibrated with a low murmuring, like a whispered conversation just audible but not decipherable. Sibilant, sighing, it exuded triumph and hate. And then, suddenly, as if someone had closed a soundproof door on it, it was gone.

They scanned each other's faces, read that their companions too had heard it. Meredith drew in a deep breath.

'Let's get into the lounge.'

They rejoined Carol, Ann and Joyce. Ann, in tears, was being comforted by Joyce. Carol seized Paul's hand as he crossed to sit beside her. Her own cheeks were wet with recent tears, her hand was icy.

A bitter and acrimonious debate developed, polarized about Meredith and Bourne. Stubbornly, Bourne resisted Meredith's suggestion that the deaths were anything other than accidental.

'The wooden frame of the dome was obviously rotten with age. The weight of snow, lead and glass was too much for it. It was a tragic coincidence that Swanson and Fletcher were carrying the camera equipment down the stairs when it occurred.'

'And the sounds?'

'Who knows what sounds may not be set up by a wind in such circumstances? Meredith, I will not be stampeded into acceptance of a supernatural origin or of some preposterous plot from the Other Side' – his scathing tones seared – 'to kill or injure us. I am a scientist. I go by the facts. I subscribe to Occam's Razor.'

'It may yet cut your throat,' Meredith rejoined grimly. A spasm of self-disgust twisted his face as he realized how unfortunately apposite his words were. 'I'm sorry. I shouldn't have said that.'

'I think we should leave,' said Ann abruptly. Bourne bestowed on her a 'my dear young lady, your opinion carries no weight with me' look.

It turned out that Joyce supported her. Hunt was not sure.

Paul was conscious of his own indecision, his mind tugged by a desire to ensure safety for Carol and himself and a shivering reluctance to huddle blanket-clad in the back of the car in the snow. He heard Pollard chip in.

'Of course there's no need for everyone to go with the majority wish. I suggest that we each decide. Any who wish to spend the night in the cars will be helped by the others to make themselves as comfortable as possible. For myself,' he grinned ruefully, 'I shall stay. Out of cowardice. I fear the thought of what my chaps would think if they learned I'd quit a house because of spooks. How about you, Ted?'

'You don't leave me much choice, do you? I'll stay.'

With a dull leaden feeling of foreboding, Meredith saw the lure of creature comforts and the mind's gift for rationalization winning the day. He couldn't really blame them. Bourne's explanation of the dome's collapse could well be the correct one. And yet, even while he listened to himself agree to stay in the house that night, he felt his conviction deepen that they were making the wrong decision.

They agreed that the women should go and prepare a meal even although they all professed to have no appetite. The men would try to clear away the blood-soaked debris piled up in the hall, scattered across the stairs in the futile frenzy of the attempt to save Fletcher and Swanson.

They set to work, using pails, mops and brooms found in the scullery, carrying everything down to the dank and icy depths of the cellars. Without tarpaulins and battens of wood, it was impossible to rig up a proper awning to shelter the hall from the heavy snow falling through the black gap above it. The heavy flakes drifted downwards, illuminated by the glow from the two oil-lamps set up in the hall. The incongruity of snow falling unchecked within the core of a house produced a strange and eerie effect.

The meal was in sad contrast to the dinner the previous night. Demoralized by the tragedy, they produced little conversation. Pollard declared his intention of attempting on the morrow to get to the wrecked bridge and cross the ravine. They discussed the significance of the bottle found under the floorboard upstairs.

Normally it would have been the object of intense speculative interest, in a real sense a triumphant achievement of the regression technique. Now it seemed like Dead Sea fruits, obtained at far too heavy a price. For in everyone's mind was the knowledge that as they ate down here, upstairs in the icy dark bedroom directly above them lay the bodies of two of their number.

After the meal Pollard and Smith went down to the cellars to decide where best to place the explosives for demolition. Hunt and Meredith assisted the women to wash up. Bourne and Paul made up fires, checked oil-lamps and filled hot-water bottles. There had been little argument, even from Bourne, when Meredith proposed a duty roster of people to keep watch throughout the night from eleven to eight a.m.

It was agreed that two people would be stationed in both lounge and dining-room. A pair would patrol the house every half-hour, staggering their patrols so that the house would be inspected every quarter-hour. The watches would run from eleven to two, two to five and five to eight. Bourne was odd man out as usual. He insisted on watching alone, reiterating his belief that it was almost certainly a waste of time.

There had been some argument about Ann and Joyce watching together and patrolling the house. Pollard suggested that he should watch with Ann while Hunt teamed with Joyce. Neither girl would hear of it since it would have meant that one of them would be sleeping alone. While they obviously loathed the thought of patrolling the house, it seemed less unbearable than being left alone in their bedroom. Paul caught Carol nodding slowly in understanding, her face taut with recollection. It was finally agreed that Paul would patrol every fifteen minutes with either Carol, Ann or Joyce during their spell of duty.

At this point in the discussion, with their plans laid out with military-style precision, they hesitated, their eyes searching each other's faces. Paul wondered if they were all thinking much the same thing. In this last quarter of the twentieth century, in a supposedly post-superstitious, post-religious, materialistic age, a group of people had largely convinced themselves of the necessity of watching out for 'things that went bump in the night'.

It was absurd. It was utterly ludicrous. And yet . . . He remembered the man upstairs, the noises, the weeping, the physical phenomena, Carol's story, the Mary Rolfe entity. And Fletcher and Swanson's enigmatic deaths. And he saw Meredith's haunted face. What was he really afraid of?

Pollard grinned briefly.

'I know. I can see you thinking: are we being complete idiots? Well, perhaps so. On the other hand remember the immortal words: If you can keep your head, when all about you are losing theirs, then it may be you just haven't assessed the situation correctly, my son!' And his gaze switched to Arnold Bourne. 'If we get a peaceful night we can afford to laugh at ourselves tomorrow.'

16   Inferno

In the lounge the fire sagged. A flame, blue-hot, rose phoenix-like from the glowing red heart of the partially consumed logs. The slight noise brought Paul's head up and he glanced at his watch. Three-twelve. Almost time to make the next round. He looked across at Carol, huddled in a corner of the couch. He got up to position another log on the fire. When they had come downstairs she had sat beside him on his couch, his arms about her. But she had seemed uneasy and finally admitted she couldn't stand having both their backs towards the battened doors of the billiards-room.

'All right,' he had said. 'You sit opposite me. You watch my back and I'll watch yours.'

When they had retired at eleven they had lain at first in each other's arms, hesitant about making love, both of them conscious of the room along the corridor, of the two bodies lying under their white sheets. To love seemed quite irrationally improper in such circumstances; it seemed an affront to the dead somehow. But then necessity overtook them. On the previous night their love-making had been driven by a single-minded need for each other, tonight it had been an affirmation of life itself, a light and a warmth in the enclosing darkness of Ardvreck House. Afterwards, in the post-coital spell, he had searched her wide eyes, found them tear-filled.

'I'm sorry,' she said. 'I can't help thinking of us and then think-ing of them . . .' He had stroked the back of her head, not know-ing what to say.

Now in the lounge he straightened up from the fire. Crossing to Carol he bent and kissed her.

'Time to move.'

She rose. Paul opened the lounge door. The icy cold atmos-phere of the hall met him. And blackness. The oil-lamp burning there had gone out. Carol stood in the threshold watching while he crossed the mushy layer of snow, his torch beam searching the depth of the hall like a car headlamp. He removed the glass shade, turned up the wick, struck a match and relit the lamp. It burned brightly, steadying as he replaced the cover. A gust of wind or some heavier snowflakes must have put it out, he thought. The explanation did not quite convince him.

Carol closed the lounge door and joined him at the dining-room door. He opened it and they entered. He noticed that Ann and Joyce also sat on either side of the fire.

'My turn,' said Joyce and got up. She wore her red ski-outfit. Carol took her place.

Paul and Joyce, torches in hand, climbed the wet, slippery staircase to the first floor gallery. So far all seemed to be in order. As they came to the narrow, steep flight of stairs leading to the attics, Paul found himself uneasily expectant. On previous nights about this time the noises had been heard.

They ascended, the beams darting ahead like hunting dogs. Once or twice they stopped as stray rustlings, scrapings just on the threshold of audibility, came to their ears. It was impossible to pin down the directions from which these noises came. Paul fought away the idea of something, out of sight behind the wall on his left, keeping pace with them. The second time they stopped, with Joyce gripping his arm so fiercely he knew bruises would result, she breathed the one word 'Rats?' in his ear.

'Possibly,' he murmured, but did not believe it. The house had lain empty so long no rats would have remained.

Joyce pressed close behind him as they descended to the first floor again by the other stair. He knew she was thinking that there was nothing behind her back. When they came down the main staircase, they felt snowflakes settle on their heads. They crossed the wet hall and entered the dining-room.

Ann stood in front of the fire, her back to it, as taut as a migraine sufferer in the throes of an attack. Her head flicked round expectantly.

'All quiet,' Paul murmured. He saw her frown.

'I feel terrible,' she said abruptly. 'I feel utterly sure something is going to happen, something awful. I feel cold. It is cold, isn't it?'

Carol, from her seat beside the fire, looked up at her.

'Yes, it is. This fire doesn't really do anything for this room. Are you feeling ill, Ann? Do you think you have caught a chill?'

'No. It isn't that.'

'Perhaps a reaction from . . . well . . . what happened this after-noon?' Joyce suggested. There were dark shadows under her own eyes.

'No.' Ann shook her head. 'It's not . . . what's already happened. It's what's going to happen. It's worse because I don't know what's going to happen.'

'Well, everything seems quiet upstairs,' Paul repeated.

'But you didn't go into the empty rooms,' she accused.

'Well, no. But they're secure.' He almost flinched from the look of bleak dismissal on her face.

'How about some coffee?' he suggested. 'Remember I've got to do the rounds again in fifteen minutes' time.'

She laughed brittlely, her eyes mocking his attempt to occupy her.

'All right, I'll make some.'

She broke off. Her head turned. From the direction of the kitchen a slithering sound had come. Their eyes staring at the closed double doors, the four listened intently. Behind the doors the slithering was repeated, softly and surreptitiously. And a heavy metallic, hollow thud was heard, familiar to Paul, agoniz-ingly so because he could not place it. A scraping sound followed.

It seemed to Paul as if his spinal fluid had been replaced by ice-water. A wave of fear passed over him like a chill breeze from the roofless hall. Was it his imagination or did one of the doors actually ease towards them a little as if under a cautious, testing pressure from the other side?

There were more noises; a trundling sound which lasted all of four seconds was succeeded by a fresh bout of scraping and scratching. Somehow he managed to take the first step towards the kitchen doors.

'What are you going to do?' Joyce hissed.

'Open them.'

'No!' Carol was on her feet by now.

'They may only be noises.'

'No. Don't open the doors.' Ann stared at them, her face white.

He thought feverishly: if it's just another example of this unquiet house's tricks . . . But even as he thought that he realized with a fresh surge of fear that at that last thud, the left-hand door had sagged forward a shade.

'Ann, Joyce, Carol.' A tiny part of him marvelled that his voice was steady. 'Go upstairs and waken the others. Go on.'

There was another muffled rap. It seemed to change direction swiftly during its existence, seemed latterly to have a source within the dining-room. The women hesitated.

'Go on!' he urged.

Like sleep-walkers they approached the door to the hall, heads still turned towards the kitchen doors. Joyce stopped, her hand on the door-knob. An uncontrollable fit of trembling seized her. Her voice was low but distinctly audible.

'Oh God! Oh God! Suppose I open this door and it's there waiting outside in the hall – ' She found herself utterly paralysed by the thought that whatever it was it might have circled round via the butler's pantry and be waiting for them to emerge. She had never known that it was possible to feel such horror and avoid fainting.

Paul read her anguish, saw it spread to Ann and Carol. Somewhere deep inside him anger born of outrage seized him. It nerved him to stride to the kitchen doors. Taking a deep, trembling breath he seized the handle, turned it and pushed. The door did not budge. It was the last thing he had expected. He put all his strength behind his next attempt. The solid door creaked but did not give. Over his shoulder he cast a startled glance at the girls.

'It won't move. Either it's locked or – '

He looked down. There was no keyhole visible.

'We'd better get the others.'

He found his scalp creep as the thought struck him that perhaps the door to the hall was also held shut. He strode past the women, was about to attempt to open it when a renewed outburst of noise came from beyond the kitchen doors. A high-pitched cry of terror slashed the listeners' eardrums. It was immediately followed by the scrabble of running footsteps. A body or at least something heavy seemed to be hurled at the kitchen doors so that they shook under the thunderous assault. And then with utterly nerve-racking effect, sustained shrieks of terror were heard, the protests of someone driven beyond the edge of reason, pitched so high that it was impossible to decide if they originated from man or woman. They died away as if a poor wretch was being dragged screaming to the fires of Hell.

Paul found himself scraping the back of his hand across his jaw. His teeth were ground together, his lips drawn back. Ann and Joyce gripped each other, their trembling so extreme it was probable they found difficulty in standing upright. Carol's eyes showed white all round her staring pupils. Her hands gripped the sides of her head, the fingers buried in her hair. Her teeth chattered.

Paul seized himself mentally by the scruff of the neck. He tried the door to the hall. It came inwards. Outside the hall was dark again. The oil-lamp was out once more. A moving light at the top of the stair caught his searching eye. Pollard's voice came from the gallery.

'What in God's name was that? Wilson, are you all right down there?'

'Pollard! Waken everyone. Get them down here.'

He heard Pollard call to someone. Panting as fiercely as if he had been sprinting, he sent his torch beam along the dark passageway beside the staircase that led to the rear premises. There was another entrance to the kitchen down there. Was it also held shut against them? It was certain he wasn't going to test it until the others had come down to join him. He knew he should cross the hall to light the lamp again – why did it keep going out? – but again he held his ground at the threshold to the dining-room. Behind him the women pressed against him. He knew they would be keeping an eye on the double doors leading to the kitchen. Carol was pressed so closely against him that he could feel the violent trembling of her body.

Pollard was coming downstairs now, his own torch-beam lighting up the slushy treads. He reached the foot of the stairs. Paul experienced a surge of relief, realized how near to breaking-point he had been. Pollard darted a glance at him, crossed the hall, lifted off the glass cover of the oil-lamp and relit the wick. The warm glow was one of the most pleasant sights Paul had seen for long enough. A snatch of St John's Gospel surfaced in his mind. 'For everyone that doeth evil hateth the light, neither cometh to the light . . .' God! He hadn't thought of that since he was a boy.

Someone else was descending the stairs. Paul saw that it was Meredith, addressed Pollard.

'There's something in the kitchen. Those screams came from there.' He quickly explained the situation with the doors. Meredith arrived to listen without interruption. By the time Paul had finished, Smith and Hunt were also on the stairs. Finally Bourne appeared.

They stood in a group on either side of the threshold, Paul, Smith and Meredith within the room, beside the table facing the double doors, the girls just within the room. In the hall Pollard, Hunt and Bourne faced the passageway leading to the back premises and the other entrance to the kitchen. With a sick numbness in his stomach Paul realized that whatever it was that had been in the kitchen could already have escaped while he and the girls were in the dining-room. Before any of the other men had come downstairs it could have slipped upstairs and be in hiding anywhere in the house.

Paul and Smith approached the double doors knowing that Pollard and Hunt would be advancing cautiously along the passage towards the other door. Paul glanced at Smith and pressed his ear to the panel near the division. Beside him Smith did likewise, his strained face towards Paul's. There was nothing to be heard. Moistening his lips, Paul turned the door knob and pushed. The door creaked but otherwise resisted his pressure. Smith applied his own shoulder to the other door but made no impression.

Someone called from the corridor. Meredith listened intently, turned towards them.

'The other door's stuck too. Do you detect any light in the kitchen?'

Smith put his eye to the division between the doors.

'No.' He gazed at the doors. 'On TV they never have any difficulty in forcing doors. One good shove with the shoulder and in it goes.' He bit at a fingernail. 'Look, suppose we give it a try. Count of three and we give it all we've got. You take the left; I'll take the right. We might force it. Okay?'

Paul nodded.

'Just a moment.' He crossed to Meredith, let him know what they planned. Meredith in turn passed word round to Hunt and Pollard, suggested that he himself should give the countdown for a simultaneous assault by Paul and Smith on the double doors and by Hunt and Pollard on the passage door.

They positioned themselves about a yard from the doors. Meredith raised his voice.

'On the count of zero. Three. Two. One. Zero!'

Paul and Smith hurled themselves at the doors. Paul felt his left shoulder and upper arm thud painfully against the dingy brown panels in unison with Smith's effort. Both men gasped with the shock. Breathing heavily they straightened up, saw that their efforts had met with some success. There was a two inch wide vertical gap of darkness between the door edges now. Smith strode to the table, picked up a torch, shone it through the gap.

'There's all sorts of things piled up here. That's what's holding the doors. Come on, let's give them another shove!'

Again Paul's aching shoulder struck the door. This time he heard a grinding, creaking noise as the objects behind it were displaced a few more inches. The gap was a foot wide now. Even as he recognized that the barricade against the doors included the old-fashioned heavy kitchen table and a six-foot-tall massive double-doored cupboard, he heard Meredith call out that the men in the corridor were having some success. Through the gap he saw torchlight from the corridor splash through the pitch darkness beyond the barrier.

His eyes shining in triumph, Smith put his back to the partially open right-hand door and heaved. The cupboard tilted, hung for a moment then toppled to fall with a resounding crash on the kitchen floor. It was easier then to push away the table lying on its side and prise open the kitchen doors fully. Almost at the same time Pollard and Hunt managed to squeeze through the gap in their doorway and enter the icy kitchen.

Lamplight combined with the torch beams to illuminate a scene of insane chaos. Apart from the fallen cupboard, the upturned table and the cupboard contents – pots, pans, cups, saucers, plates, tins and packets of food – the old cooker, fridge and washing machine had also been displaced. The washing machine stood on top of the cooker, both pieces of kitchen equipment having barred entrance to the kitchen by the passage doorway.

Silently the four men shone their torches about. Many of the food packets had burst. A number of the tins had been crumpled and even torn open. Pools of syrup held half-peaches and apricots, resembling eggs freshly broken from their shells. Mounds of beans gleamed oilily amid broken packets of biscuits.

Grimly Pollard directed his torch beam to the door leading to the scullery. It was closed. At the same time Paul became conscious of two things – the stench of calor gas and the fact that he could not see the portable stove or the two big calor-gas cylinders. And he realized that he now recognized the hollow clanking sound he had heard as the sound a gas cylinder makes when it hits a stone floor.

A premonition of danger brought a prickling sensation to the back of his neck. What lay behind the scullery door? Had whatever it was retreated from the kitchen to the scullery? The kitchen became fully illuminated as Meredith brought an oil lamp into it. He surveyed the debris, the lamp held at head level. Bourne appeared at the other door, his expression one of amazed disbelief and distaste. Paul glanced over his shoulder through the doorway to the dining-room. There Ann, Joyce and Carol stared in stupefaction at the scene of devastation within the kitchen. He turned back. Pollard's hand was on the door knob of the scullery door. The set of his back screamed his tension. He rotated the knob and pushed. The door opened easily. And the smell of gas increased in strength. A deadly hissing sound came to their ears. Pollard coughed chestily.

'The scullery's full of it,' he called.

He stepped back. A wave of cold as if the door of a deep-freeze had been opened swept over the kitchen bringing with it the overpowering stench of the gas. Meredith approached Pollard.

'Where are the gas cylinders? Do you see them?'

'No. I can't. They could be in the scullery. It's pitch black in there. They could be under the old sinks. But one at least is leaking.'

'Or turned on.' Meredith's voice was bleak.

Pollard coughed again.

'Get everyone out of here into the dining-room. I've got to find the cylinders and turn the gas off.'

Paul and Smith moved forward to help Pollard. Meredith shouted to the others to move back. Smith slipped on a pool of peach juice and nearly fell. Pollard was now back in the scullery. Paul took a deep breath and joined him in the freezing cold, stinking atmosphere. Quickly they searched the scullery before retreating again to the kitchen. There they took in gasping breaths. And all the time the hissing continued.

'They must be downstairs,' Pollard muttered. His troubled eyes stared at Paul and Smith. The latter swore.

'How could they get down there?'

'Never mind that. The point is that if we can smell it so strongly up here, the cellars must be full of it. God knows how long it's been building up there. It's heavier than air. This place is a potential bomb.' He sucked in his breath sharply. 'Oh my God! The dining-room fire! Quick! Everybody out of the house. Now! Before the place goes up.'

'Can't we try –' Smith began.

'No time! Everybody out! Through the front door.'

His sense of extreme urgency communicated itself to the others. Paul's chilled mind imagined the unseen tide of calor gas rising within the kitchen, rising until it began to spill over on to the higher dining-room floor, swirling menacingly across towards the fire-place where the leaping flames waited to ignite it. Recollections of accounts he had read of cabin cruisers blown to matchwood by the explosion of calor gas leaked into their bilges flashed across his mind. He helped to hustle the others out of the dining-room into the wet hall. Meredith produced the keys and unlocked the door, fumbling once before he opened it.

A gust of wind and sleet slapped their faces. The women hesitated. It still seemed absurd to leave the house's shelter and go out into the night.

'Go on!' Meredith shouted.

The women were down the steps running towards the vehicles, the men following when flash-point came. The world seemed to explode. Paul got one glimpse of the vehicle sides starkly lit up as if by lightning at the same time that he was seized by the gigantic hand of the blast and hurled towards them. He fell heavily among the women, now prone in the snow beside the van. Almost deaf, he faintly heard screams and shouts. Wet snow seeped coldly through his clothes as he lay there, dazed and semi-conscious. The darkness was attacked by flickering lights, there was a crashing and crackling noise and the world seemed on fire.

17   The Final Secret

He tried to move, his battered mind screaming Carol's name. He raised himself on an elbow, gasping as pain stabbed his left wrist.

An inferno faced him. Great crimson gouts of flame shot from shattered window-frames, leaping skywards, sending waves of heat towards him. A continual roar came from the fire as it spread quickly through the old house, feeding voraciously on its timbers and contents.

He climbed to his feet, swaying, conscious of the fierce breath of the conflagration on his face and the chill of his soaking clothes. Others, dark figures between him and the golden-red backdrop of flames, were sprawled, or were sitting up or were shakily getting to their feet.

Ann was helping Joyce to her feet. Their figures were garishly illuminated. Neither seemed hurt but were obviously shocked. Where was Carol? His heart thumped within him as he saw her body lying yards away. He staggered across, dropped to his knees beside her, saw in a glory of relief that she was moving her head and arms. She recognized him, raised her head. He cradled it gently on his arm.

'Are you all right?'

He watched, the fire's warmth hot on his back, as she moved her arms and legs. She seemed unhurt.

He raised her to her feet. They backed towards the vehicles. He saw Pollard and Smith supporting Bourne between them. Meredith unlocked the Volvo, opened the rear door. Pollard and Smith manoeuvred Bourne's body on to the seat. Ann examined a deep gash on his head, attempted to staunch the copious bleeding with a clean handkerchief. Even as she worked, Bourne recovered consciousness.

They had got off extraordinarily lightly, Paul thought. He knew already his left wrist was broken. Bourne might show concussion effects later and had a head wound that probably required stitching. But apart from that they seemed unhurt. He looked at Ardvreck House, roasting in its own funeral pyre, remembered the colossal power of the explosion and shivered.

If they had delayed a minute longer before quitting the house. Or if they had not been keeping watch throughout the night. He thought of them sleeping upstairs while that thing with its diabolical power heaped up its barricade of kitchen furniture, moved the gas cylinders to the cellars and turned them on. None of them would have escaped alive.

With his arm around Carol he watched the flames consume the house. In the furnace heat snow melted and cascaded as water from the roof. The wet gravel of the driveway was fast appearing from beneath its retreating coat of white. The fire had a grip on the second floor now. Sheets of flame were pouring from the bedroom windows; the roar of the conflagration was louder.

Pollard approached them, shouting something.

'We'd better get the cars farther down the drive. If the front of the house falls outwards – '

He nodded, was about to search for his keys when he froze. A gust of wind parted the smoke, revealing the windows of the tower room. To his horror he saw a figure at the window gazing down at them, the same figure of the clean-shaven burly man he had seen on the morning Carol and he had tried to get away from the house. Hands behind his back, the figure at the window stood motionless and impassive while smoke and flames billowed past him.

'Pollard! Look!' He seized Pollard's arm, almost dragging the army man round while he tried to point with his left. Pollard's breath hissed in. Paul knew with strangely mixed feelings of satisfaction and fear that Pollard also saw the figure. He too saw a man stand at a window ringed with flames, in a furnace heat where no living thing could have survived.

Suddenly the first floor collapsed. The thunder of its fall was followed by the renewed roar of the inferno as it attacked the upper part of the house. The windows still unbroken were exploding outwards. A solid wall of flame shot from the tower windows and the figure was gone.

Reports like pistol shots heralded the first flames bursting through the roof of the house. Pollard looked up. Dislodged slates were pouring over the eaves in a deadly black rain.

'Come on, let's get moving.'

Surprisingly, none of the cars proved difficult to start. Five minutes later the small convoy had halted a hundred yards away from the doomed house. It was bitterly cold there though the cars were sheltered by the belt of trees. Even so, most of the men and women, wrapped in blankets, stood outside for an hour silently watching the fire's further progress, the thought of Fletcher and Swanson's bodies lying heavy on their minds.

The grey watered light of dawn saw the group restored to some kind of order. The Volvo's first-aid box had provided material for strapping up Paul's wrist. Bourne's head had been properly bandaged. Coffee had been made on the portable calor gas stove. They had even had hot soup.

It was doubtful if anyone had done more than doze all through the remainder of the night. About six o'clock heavy rain had begun to fall, drumming on the car roofs, running down the steamed-up windows. It slackened after an hour, stopped at eight-fifteen. When they wearily opened the car doors, got out and stretched themselves they noticed that the bitter winter chill had gone. It was still cold and damp, but with the temperature obviously well above freezing. Already the snow was turning to slush. In the Ardnamurchan hills the gullies would be foaming torrents. It was almost as if the destruction of Ardvreck House had broken some spell it had cast over the winter landscape.

Paul looked across at the blackened, smoking ruin. The walls still stood on the sides nearer the cars. Greasy grey smoke wafted desultorily upwards to the brightening sky like smoke from a town's rubbish dump. Paul sniffed, detecting even at one hundred yards, the sour, harsh stench a burned house exudes.

Pollard crossed to him. He looked tired and strained. Like many red-haired men his beard would be blond, judging by the stubble on his chin.

'How's the arm?'

'It'll do.'

'Good. If this improvement in the weather keeps up some of us should be able to get help by nightfall.'

'When are you thinking of moving?'

'Almost immediately. We'll take the Land-Rover, try to clear the road to the bridge. After that it'll be on foot. Smith and Hunt will come with me.' He grimaced. 'I know it seems like most of the able-bodied are quitting but I don't see any other way. There are probably umpteen drifts on the road and it'll be hard going on foot when we get across the gully.'

Paul grinned, sketched a salute.

'Aye, aye, Captain. Don't worry. We'll be all right. Somehow I think Ardvreck House has no more surprises for us.'

He could not have been more wrong.

About half an hour later the Land-Rover left, with Smith driving. Paul turned to Carol. From the look on her face she obviously did not know whether to be glad they had gone for help or to be apprehensive because the group was further weakened. He squeezed her arm.

'It's all over, darling. A few hours more and we'll be on our way.'

'A honeymoon to remember,' she said quietly.

'I'm not sure I want to.'

'Indeed!'

'Well, let's say I intend my memories to be very selective.'

'Oh?'

'And reinforced by frequent repetition.'

The corner of her mouth twitched.

'Oh yes. Well, if you plan to come back here you can come alone.'

He saw Bourne and Meredith arguing beside the van. Meredith looked desperately tired, his fleshy face sagging. Arnold Bourne, with the bandage round his dark head, looked equally exhausted but seemed as positive as ever. Paul raised his eyebrows at Carol, left her to walk over to them. Meredith turned to him.

'Bourne wants to walk round the house.'

'What! Go inside?'

Bourne shook his head, winced.

'No of course not. Highly dangerous, I should imagine. No, I merely wish to walk round the outside, have a look at what the fire's done.' He hesitated, lowered his voice. 'In any case, I feel we should see if there are any signs of Fletcher and Swanson's bodies.'

Paul felt his stomach uneasy. He glanced at the ruin.

'Would there be anything left?'

'Not much, I should think,' Meredith interjected. 'Really, Bourne, haven't you realized by now that we should keep well away from that place?'

It was the wrong thing to say. Paul saw Bourne's mouth tighten.

'Very well, I'll go by myself.'

In the event the three men agreed to walk round the ruined house. Neither Meredith nor Paul could let Bourne venture by himself near the building and he would not give up the idea. The women, appreciating what the men might find, had no desire to accompany them.

As they approached what had once been the front of the house, the incinerator smell strengthened. They walked along the bare gravel drive, avoiding the piles of shattered slates, the fallen stonework and charred black timbers fallen from the roof. The nearest snow was all of thirty yards away, so fierce had been the heat.

In the quiet April morning, their feet seemed to crunch unnecessarily loudly over the gravel.

The pillared portico was still in place but framed a rectangular gap where the front door had been. Every floor had been consumed. When they reached the east end of the front and turned left, the full extent of the destruction was revealed. The east wall had fallen outwards. Most of the internal walls had vanished or had been reduced to bare brick. A tangle of smoking debris filled the cellar area, heaped up to various heights, with black, crooked fingers of half-consumed beams sticking up at crazy angles. Possibly, Paul thought, the heavy downpour of rain had helped to prevent their total consumption by the flames. He raised his eyes, traced along the inside of the front wall the regular indentations where once the first-floor main beams had had their ends embedded in the stonework. There had been the floor of the bedroom, just there had stood the bed. . . . As Carol had remarked, a honeymoon to remember.

The three men walked on slowly, picked their way over rubble fallen out from the scullery. The cellar underneath it was also filled by debris. Paul noted one of the old-fashioned sinks half-sunk in the rubble. They turned left again round what had been the back of the house and the small overgrown yard between scullery and ruined conservatory. So far none of the three men had made any comment to any of the others. Paul felt depression heavy on his mind. The sordid scene of violent destruction by fire seemed no more than a fitting end to Ardvreck House's history of treachery, murder, suicide and hate. He wondered if Pollard would still bring his men to finish the job with explosives. Even if every trace of the house were removed and the vegetation allowed to grow over the area, he thought it more than likely that any sensitive person visiting the spot in the future would still feel the sombre, brooding tones of misery and terror that lingered on.

He saw Bourne look up at the place on the east wall where bedroom number six had been then look downwards into the heaped-up debris. Meredith stood beside him, also scanning the debris. Paul, his stomach like cold lead, walked towards them. Reluctantly he examined the jumbled interior. But there was no sign of the blackened shrivelled things he feared to see.

Bourne and Meredith's eyes met. As if some unspoken message passed between them, they moved on. Paul followed them. They moved round the semicircular end of the ruined conservatory. More of the rusty, ornate wrought-iron pillars had collapsed bringing down a large part of the remaining structure. Meredith and Bourne were now walking down the littered path beside the western side of the destroyed billiards-room. Paul blinked. A strange alteration in his state of mind had taken place. He was aware of an increased alertness almost reminiscent of the return to sharp sobriety after the warm slightly out of focus state induced by alcohol has worn off. Time seemed to have slowed.

He halted.

Something made him turn his head slightly to the left. In the gap that had once been the door from the billiards-room to the conservatory stood the figure of a girl, solid and real. She wore a proud little toque hat, a grey-green jacket, waisted with a short flaring skirt, and a long, ankle-length skirt of the same colour, widening all the way to the ground. Below the jacket was a white, high-collared, frilly blouse. She stood, neither sideways nor facing him, only her pale, heart-shaped face turned towards him. Her expression was one of extreme and tragic sadness, and appeal.

It seemed to him that their eyes met across the air above the ruined conservatory and across time. He wanted to move towards her, to call out to the others. But he was afraid the movement or sound would dispel the situation. And he was utterly sure that the only thing that mattered was to help her.

He had no idea how long he stood there. Meredith and Bourne were out of sight now, behind the lounge wall. He drew a deep, slow breath and moved a step forward. She remained visible, quite motionless. He was almost standing against the battered, waist-high stonework that formerly had supported the curved glass wall of the conservatory. Slowly he placed his right hand on the rough top of the grey sandstone. He looked down. With his broken wrist and arm in a sling it was going to be a bit of a struggle to get over. His glance flicked up. She was still there. Leaning on his right hand he bent forward, raised his left leg to the top of the stonework, brought up his right leg and managed to cross. He straightened up.

His heart was pounding, he saw that the figure of the girl was drifting away into the billiards-room. He followed it, crunching over tiles and broken glass. A piece of stone that had once formed part of a kerb separating path from plants caused him to stumble, to look down. When he recovered and looked across at the doorway he found that she had gone. He scrambled across the uneven, debris-bestrewn ground, came to the doorway and halted.

The floor of the billiards-room had been destroyed in the fire so that the big storeroom in the cellars below now lay open to the sky. Most of its floor was buried deeply in mounds of tiles, charred roof-beams, plaster fragments, stones and bricks, but the area against the outside wall of the house had escaped burial completely. Paul looked down into its depths and stiffened, a wave of horror and sickness sweeping over him.

'Oh Christ,' he murmured, his brow cold and wet with sweat. Ardvreck House had given up its last secret.

18   Devil in the Darkness

Meredith and Bourne stood beside him, looking at what had been disclosed by the destruction of the billiards-room floor. At his cry they had hurried back. With a trembling hand, Meredith took a handkerchief across the lower part of his face.

About three feet from the outside wall of the house a second brick wall stood parallel to it forming a cavity that stretched the full length of the cellar storeroom. The second wall must once have divided off the cavity from the rest of the cellars, stretching up to the ceiling of the basement premises. Outside it, in the store-room, most of the debris had fallen, burying the storeroom to within three feet of the former ceiling. Some beams, crashing down from above, had jammed themselves across the brick wall and shielded the three-foot-wide cavity from most of the falling debris. Water from melting pipes had also flooded it to a depth of four feet, further helping to preserve its contents from the full ferocity of the fire.

Paul looked into the cavity. His eyes seemed drawn to its contents. Mercifully the filthy water surface concealed most of the interior. He found his mind in a turmoil of distressed half-formed speculations. Beside him Arnold Bourne moved forward.

'What are you going to do?' asked Meredith.

'Get down to the surface of the debris for a closer look.'

Meredith glanced at Paul but said nothing. They watched intently as Bourne eased himself down through the gap on to the piled-up debris, testing its bearing strength before resting his full weight on it. It resettled itself a little, creaking and clattering.

Smoke rose lazily from it like a swarm of bees from a disturbed hive. Bourne, one hand on the inside of the wall that formerly had been the back of the house, edged his way across the four feet of wildly irregular surface separating him from the broken brick wall. He grabbed at the wall, lurched as a section broke off and finally finished leaning against it, the upper half of his body almost over it. Concentric rings spread out across the water surface from the place where the brick section had splashed into the flooded cavity. Some bubbles rose, burst, and something else surfaced to float, almost submerged.

Bourne stared at it. He leant precariously over the broken wall and found he could touch it with outstretched hand. At the second attempt he managed to hold it and lift it dripping from the greasy water. Carefully he made his way back to the others, handed it up to them and climbed up after it.

Meredith turned it over in his hands. As far as Paul could see it was a small once-black deedbox, no more than ten inches by five inches by four. Its surface was roughened and reddened with rust. On its top was a ring, now rusted immovably to the top. Where there should have been a keyhole, a metal plate had been fixed to the side.

'As far as I can see,' Bourne said, 'there are only two reasonable hypotheses. Either it existed in the house upstairs and fell into that cavity when the house collapsed during the fire or it already was in the cavity when the fire began.'

Meredith nodded.

'Presumably the part of the wall you pushed into the water dislodged what was holding it down.' He took a deep breath. 'I suggest we get back to the cars and try to find some way of opening this. Whatever is in it may tell us which of your hypotheses is the correct one.'

The three men walked down the drive towards the car. The women stood by the television van looking towards them, obviously anxious because they had taken so long to reappear. They knew immediately by the expressions on the men's faces that something had happened. Paul, unable to work on the box, told them what they had found while the other men brought out the van's tool kit.

'In the cellars?' Joyce repeated. 'But you searched the cellars. You didn't find anything then.'

Carol, her face white with horror, looked at him.

'You think the other wall was built to conceal them?' Her eyes narrowed as he made no reply. 'There's something else, isn't there?'

He nodded, swallowed bile as he remembered.

'I'm not sure.' But in his own mind he had no doubts.

'Was it done recently?' Ann asked, her voice higher-pitched.

'Impossible to say at the moment. Dr Bourne wouldn't commit himself. Said he had no forensic experience.' He hesitated. 'I think it happened many years ago.' A vision of the tragic-faced girl in her turn of the century clothes rose before him. Carol looked at him.

'Why do you think that?'

Quietly he told them of the appearance of the girl and of how she seemed to have drawn his attention to the cavity and its contents.

The sound of metallic blows drew his attention. Bourne and Meredith were using a hammer and chisel on the deedbox. It was not so deeply rusted as they had thought and did not seem to have been locked. Before long the lid had been wrenched off far enough for them to see what appeared to be brown parchment inside. At length Bourne signed to Meredith to cease his efforts. He picked up the box from the wet gravel and placed it on the bonnet of the Volvo. Inserting his hand he gently withdrew a sheaf of papers from the box. While the others crowded around him he examined his find.

Their first impression that there was parchment was a false

one. The papers in the sheaf were quarto in size. The whole sheaf had been folded once before placing it in the box and it was the two outer sheets that had been scorched brown by the heat and rendered brittle. Probably only its submersion in water had saved the box's contents from being roasted out of existence. Very delicately Bourne separated the inner sheets from the scorched pair and unfolded them. Paul and the others saw that they were covered with neat handwriting, the ink being scarcely faded.

Bourne looked up.

'I suggest, since it's still quite chilly, that we get into the Volvo. And then I think the best thing I can do it to read it out to you all. All right?'

They nodded. They climbed in, Meredith taking the driver's seat, Paul beside him. The three girls took the bench seat while Bourne seated himself on some blankets behind the bench seat, the box placed beside him. As he finished each sheet of paper he took it from the sheaf and placed it down gently on one of the folded blankets. His voice was steady and clear and his listeners, apart from occasional intakes of breath, heard him to the end in silence.

*   *   *   *   *

Ardvreck House

28 August 1895

Sooner or later this house's days will be ended and it will be demolished. For no house stands for ever. And when this happens, what I have done will be discovered. It could be that at some future date repairs to the cellars will be required, or extensions will be made. There are a number of possibilities that may, if any of them occurs, cause the house's secret to be revealed long before its life is over.

However it happens I want no one else to be blamed for what I have done. That is why I have written this account – not to justify my actions. I know that there are many who would condemn me and perhaps they are right. But I have no regrets. I have done many things for which I feel regret but not this.

My name is Peter Simon Cavendish, only son of Colonel Edward Cavendish of Marks Hall, Taunton. I was born on November 18th 1862. My only sister Elaine was born on February 12th, 1870.

I received an excellent education. My father wanted me to follow him into the army, into his own regiment, if possible, but army life had no appeal for me. I was, in short, a great disappointment to my father and a source of great distress to my mother who found herself witness to the many rows her menfolk inflicted upon her.

The upshot of it was that after a particularly violent altercation, I decided it was time to get out. I was twenty at the time. I rather liked what I had heard of South Africa so I gathered what cash I had and sailed for Cape Town.

For the next six years I made my way in Africa. When I reached it, it was in even more of a ferment than it is now. Cetewayo's Zulus had not long been defeated. The land was wide open. I operated in Cape Colony, moved to the Transvaal, to Natal, in fact to wherever I felt drawn to. I did everything, risked my neck in various enterprises, some within the law, some outside. I hunted, traded, explored, prospected for gold and diamonds.

Whenever I could I wrote mother or Elaine. I tried to make my letters optimistic, interesting and reassuring and I think I succeeded, judging by the few I received at various accommodation addresses I used.

Occasionally Elaine would slip in photographs of the family. If these pictures did not lie, she was growing into a regular beauty and in her letters I thought I detected traces of the restless spirit that had driven me to South Africa.

I made one trip home, in 1888. Elaine had written me telling me that she was engaged to be married, that the date fixed for the wedding was June 16th, that it would complete her happiness if her brother could be present at the ceremony.

I was flush at the time; in fact I was now very well off. The letter had reached me well in advance of the date. I did want to be present when Elaine was married. I was curious to see the man who was to be her husband. And I did want to see mother again – and father. And so I wrote saying that I would be in London on business around that time.

In the Bible the prodigal got a hearty welcome from his father when he returned. I did not really expect the same treatment from father. The formal invitation I received did have, written on it by mother, the words 'Oh Peter, please accept,' and so I knew that father had not absolutely forbidden me the door. I suppose I really did not know what to expect. Nor, I suppose, did he. I think the rather hard-looking stranger who turned up, in appearance far older than his middle twenties, threw him. He was stiff at first and very formal. But over the week I stayed, we did achieve a better measure of forbearance and understanding than we had ever previously had.

Mother and Elaine were overwhelming in their welcome. The photographs had not lied. Elaine had grown into a beautiful, spirited young woman, so lovely and with such a sunny disposition it was a joy to be with her.

I was not nearly so enthusiastic about the man she was engaged to. Ronald Milne-Thompson seemed pleasant and friendly enough. His parents had both died when he was a boy and he had been brought up by his grandfather. He made his fiancée's brother welcome but there was something essentially weak in his make-up that made me uneasy. Yet Elaine was so obviously happy with him and so obviously wanted both her men to like each other that I pushed my reservations aside.

I stayed on after the ceremony for a few days then left for Africa. Apart from various interests I had there that required my attention I found that although father and I had learned to appreciate the other's point of view, we had so little in common that it would have been pointless to remain. So I booked my passage on the first available P. and O. boat and by August I was once more in Cape Town. Almost immediately I had to go up-country and it was almost a year before I returned.

The first thing that awaited me was a letter from Elaine. It was seven months old and told me that both mother and father had been carried off within a week of each other by some wretched disease. I wrote back immediately but my letter was unanswered before I had to leave Cape Town again on business.

Events in Africa in the next few years were such as to keep me occupied. I worked for Rhodes' British South Africa Company for a time, was partly instrumental in arranging the treaty with King Lobengula to enable the Matabele lands beyond the Limpopo to be exploited. My personal affairs prospered at times; at other times I seemed to be heading for disaster. Only quick thinking and a large measure of good luck enabled me to end up in 1895 with even more money than I had had in '88. It also seemed time to return to England, take a well-earned rest and look up Elaine and her husband. They were my only relations; by this time I should be an uncle several times over.

I arrived in London in March 1895. I took rooms in a hotel and began to make enquiries. And ran into a stone wall.

Milne-Thompson was no longer at the address that had been on the last letter Elaine had sent me, the one in which she had told me of our parents' deaths.

I remembered he had been something in the stock exchange. At first I drew a blank, one or two of my attempts meeting with professed ignorance or downright evasiveness. By dint of per-severance I finally found someone there who would answer my questions.

Milne-Thompson's grandfather had died in 1891 and left a considerable fortune to his grandson. He had resigned from the stock exchange, set himself up in great style. My informant told me that as far as he knew Milne-Thompson had proceeded to gamble away within two years every penny he possessed, plung-ing deeply into every vice available in London. By mid-1893 he was at the end of the line financially, physically and mentally, his excesses having alienated him from any friends he once pos-sessed. He had then committed suicide, drowning himself – in Brighton, my informant thought.

Naturally I asked about Elaine. My informant was unbear-ably vague about her – yes, if he remembered correctly, Milne-Thompson had been married at one time but that was as far as his knowledge went.

My next step was to consult the London papers of that year. The few accounts I found were damnably brief. The account of the inquest – with its verdict of suicide – gave only the sketchi-est summary of Milne-Thompson's life. His marriage was mentioned – 'married Elaine Cavendish, only daughter of the late Colonel Edward Cavendish' but gave no mention of her thereafter. It certainly did not refer to her as being called to give evidence or even make reference to her as his widow. The creepy impression I received was that the Milne-Thompsons were totally unimportant to the world, that now the formalities of the law had been completed, they would be dismissed and forgotten.

Of course I made further enquiries, even to the extent of employing private detectives. Their first reports were quite without substance. There was at least no record of the death of Mrs Ronald Milne-Thompson. In due course however they did find out that Elaine had left her husband some time before his suicide, that she had then disappeared.

Time went by and I seemed to be getting nowhere.

And then one night – even now I find it difficult to write about it; I've been sitting here for half an hour trying to summon up the resolution to go on. I had eaten with two friends from South Africa. We had seen a show, drunk rather a lot; I had shared a cab with them to their hotel, wished them goodnight. It must have been about two in the morning. Even London was asleep. I decided to walk home – I remember it was a clear night – for I wanted to think. I suppose it was a bit risky to go on foot, the route between my hotel and theirs passing through a rather sleazy district. However, I dismissed the cab and began to walk. Halfway through the district, with its long lengths of shadow between the infrequent gas lights, I began to wonder if I had been wise in paying off the cabbie.

I was almost out of that district when a drab left the shadows and accosted me. If she had seen me clearly under one of the street lights she would have hastened away but at that moment all she could have seen was a tall well-dressed gentleman, his face in shadow. To say I recognized her immediately would be a lie. Her appearance, her voice, her face had so changed that it would have been difficult for me to know who she was. It was her sharp cry of utter torment and despair when I quickly turned my head towards her and she saw my face illuminated by the nearest gaslamp that alerted me to seize her arm as she tried to retreat back into the shadows and escape.

My feelings when I recognised her are indescribable. It is sufficient to say that in one moment my whole world shattered. In the next few days I learned that Hell can come to live with you. It can live with you while you try to take care of the sister you once knew as a beautiful high-spirited young woman and who is now a diseased, broken, cocaine-addicted drab screaming for her drug, suicidal with remorse for what she has done to earn money to buy fresh supplies.

I used my money to get her into a private nursing-home, to get her the best medical attention available. I visited her at every opportunity, got her story in her lucid moments. I even began to think that there might be some chance we would restore her to health and sanity. But that was a fool's thought. About a week after I found her, she managed somehow to slash her wrists and escape into death. Now I realise that by finding her, and reawakening her spirit to whatever extent I did, I probably ensured that she would commit suicide. If I had not found her, she would have drifted on in her terrible dead way until an overdose, or pneumonia, finished off what was left of her.

I will be brief concerning her story. Inheriting his grandfather's fortune had not begun Milne-Thompson's journey to ruin. Long before that he had cashed in on his expectations, had borrowed, had drunk and gambled away everything he could lay his hands on. He had been introduced to drugs. Repelled yet trying to help her husband, Elaine, at her wits' end, had tried to enlist his remaining friends' help. They were few in number. One in particular had made every effort to tear him away from his course to final disaster. Elaine turned to this friend, confided in him. At that time he appeared a pillar of strength to her. She was utterly lonely; Ronald by this time flew into paroxysmal rages if she tried to reason with him. And in her anguish, she fell in love with her confidant. He himself revealed his own love for her. By this time her love for Ronald had died along with any respect she had left for him.

It became quite unbearable to remain any longer with her husband and she left him, going to stay with her lover. It proved the last straw for Milne-Thompson. From then on he went from bad to worse until he finally drowned himself.

Elaine remained with her lover for a few months more. He

tired of her, revealed a different side to himself. He was cruel, vicious, unscrupulous. To her horror she found out that he had been instrumental in bringing about Milne-Thompson's downfall. Wanting Elaine, he ensured that through his circle of friends her husband was given more credit, was enabled to buy more addictive drugs, was encouraged in every excess he was attracted to. In the meantime her lover played the sympathetic, charming, trustworthy friend. But that was until he was sure of her, until he became tired of her, and until he had, because of his diabolical influence over her, persuaded her too to start on the drug trail.

As her sensibilities dulled and her addiction grew, he forced her to take part in the house parties he put on for various new acquaintances he wanted to ensnare. His secretary and man-servant were as heavily involved as he was. The things that happened in that house are quite unspeakable. And she took part in them, so great was her craving by now for the drugs he could dole out to her as rewards for her cooperation. She told me these things in a tormented, compulsive manner, as if in some strange way I was her confessor and she was desperately but despairingly seeking absolution from the mortal sins she had committed. The Cavendishes are Catholic and I suppose it was her early training that prevented her from committing suicide long before I found her again. Which made it all the more terrible when she did kill herself a week after I met her.

Finally, he sold her, yes, sold her to a house in London. When she was of no further use to that house, she was kicked out. She descended the scale even further. By the time I found her she was burnt-out as a human being, existing as a dead soul.

It is almost twenty-four hours since I penned the last word. The feelings evoked by the act of writing the above account steeled me to carry out the last acts required in this damned house. Now it is time to complete my story.

The three men I determined to destroy were Arthur Bertram Howard, George Adams and William Metcalfe. I was determined that not only would I destroy them for what they had done to Elaine but I would also make them suffer, in whatever amount I could ensure, something of the pangs of Hell they had visited on my sister.

Know your enemy. That was a lesson I had learned in Africa, not only with respect to wild animals but also with respect to men. I set the best private enquiry agents I could find to the task of compiling a dossier on those three men, their appearance, acquaintances, way of life, likes and dislikes, even down to habits of dress and food. In the weeks that followed the dossier grew fat, lacunae were filled in and it became clear under such sustained and careful scrutiny of their ways that they were indeed jackals preying on the body of mankind. I steeled myself to meet Howard and cultivate his acquaintance, to encounter him in the circles he frequented, to reveal myself to him as a hard man, one who had made a considerable fortune in Africa in ways that were better hidden, in short, a man after his own heart. What is it old man Shakespeare says? 'To smile and smile, and be a villain.' I was all that.

The incredible thing is that even I felt the power of his charm. It was of course his stock-in-trade, the ability to project an aura of sincerity, of friendliness, of utter concern for the well-being of the person he was with. Some men are like that; it is as if they are born with a special faculty they can employ for good or evil. But that is by the way. As far as Howard was concerned I had only to think of Elaine to break the spell of his charm.

The Orange Free State diamond and bullion robbery gave me my chance. The papers were full of it at the time, how armed men had taken over the strongroom and made off with bullion and diamonds valued at over one million pounds sterling. Howard and I discussed it one night on the occasion I visited Ardvreck House at his invitation. He was envious of the robbers but not optimistic with respect to their chances of getting away scot-free.

'How can they hope to succeed?' he asked. 'The South African police will simply wait to see which crook begins to try to sell gold or diamonds. Or one of the four will be caught for something else and will peach on his comrades in the hope of getting off. Apart from that, there is the difficulty of getting a safe place of concealment for the gold. You cannot carry all that amount in a valise. Too bulky. And too heavy. From the accounts in the papers it must weigh at least . . . let me see . . . six tons.'

'Six tons, fifteen hundredweight,' I said.

He looked at me, his eyes narrowed. Then he laughed.

'You've been doing your homework I see.'

'And in bulk just over twelve point four cubic feet.'

'With or without boxes?' he asked slowly.

'Without. Suppose that by some means the gold – and the diamonds – were got out of the country and brought to England. Suppose the bullion was buried in a safe place and deliberately left for at least five years before being remelted and cast into ingots of a different size and shape for disposal. Would you consider that a safer proposition?'

'Why yes. Yes, indeed.' His eyes searched my face. I judged it time to play my trump card. From my jacket pocket I drew a summary of the dossier I had compiled on him and his two associates. 'Read this,' I suggested.

In the next minute I watched the blood drain from his face only to return to flush it as he read the full extent of my agents' findings. He was too sensible to deny anything. He merely sat there, tense and impassive, with murder staring out of his eyes. Watching him carefully, I went into my story.

'The original and much fuller dossier is in a sealed envelope in a bank vault. The bank directors have powers to forward it to New Scotland Yard if I fail to show up within one week or any other interval I care to specify. Now, my dear Howard, I am not threatening you. And I am giving you the opportunity to become custodian, if I may put it that way, of the bullion and the diamonds from the Kimberley mines. At the end of the agreed-upon waiting period, I am prepared to give you, Adams and Metcalfe one-seventh each of the proceeds. The other four-sevenths go to myself and my three South African associates.'

He sat there for a complete minute as if sandbagged. God alone knows what schemes, conjectures squirmed through his brain together with the lust for this enormous sum of money – at least £14,000, but more, much more if he managed to cheat us. When he began to speak, I saw that he had swallowed the bait. My story had to be true. If I was a police agent I would have turned him and his associates in, not shown him I had the evidence. Even if I was a police agent but crooked, I would have blackmailed him. As it was, I was offering him a share in the proceeds of a colossal robbery. To a man like Howard, it was only common sense that someone like myself should first of all have found out all he could about the people he was going to choose to be custodians of the loot.

He began to ask for details, to find out what I had in mind.

I told him how we had planned the robbery down to the last detail, especially with respect to the subsequent proceedings. After the robbery the gold and diamonds had been crated and slipped on board a small freighter near Port Natal. The skipper and crew thought they were shipping arms for Irish insurgents. When the freighter approached England the crates were to be transferred to a fishing-boat. Again the crew were under the impression they contained arms. My three associates travelled with the ships to oversee matters; I had come on by the fastest available P. and O. liner to find a suitable place in which to hide everything.

'You trust your colleagues to turn up?'

'I know them. I've worked with them for years. They know full well that the only real chance of us getting away with it is to carry out our original plan.' I paused. 'And they know me. They'll turn up.' I looked at him. 'Well, what do you say?'

He nodded, very slowly. If this extraordinary stroke of luck came off, all his dreams would come true. Even as we talked out the details I could see his mind constructing schemes to take possession of the entire amount. He would have to get rid of me, of course, but that he would not do until he was sure he had everything. So we arranged what he, his secretary and manservant had to do. I was to return to Ardvreck House on Monday 26th August two or three days after their preparations were completed, when the fishing boat and its bullion cargo were due.

When I reached Fort William on the afternoon of the 26th, Howard himself awaited me at the station. I had one bag with me. He took me to his coach, standing outside. I saw that the manservant Metcalfe was driving it. The journey took four hours. Howard was labouring under some excitement, as was only natural, and I had to reassure him several times that everything was going according to schedule, that the ship would arrive the following night.

When we drove up the carriageway I was shown to an upstairs bedroom. When I came downstairs again, Howard with Adams, his secretary, and Metcalfe were waiting for me in the lounge. I remember Howard's first words.

'Just as you suggested, I sent off all the servants so we will have to rough it as far as meals are concerned.'

I told him I really could not eat until I had inspected their preparations. Howard laughed.

'Just as you wish. I can understand your anxiety to see that all is in order.'

We went downstairs to the cellars, went into the big storeroom. Howard put the lamp he was carrying on a table. In its light the three men watched as I examined their work.

Across the whole of one side they had built a brick wall about three feet from the outside wall. It was complete apart from a section about four feet wide at the right-hand side through which the original back wall could be seen. Most of the new wall had already been white-washed and then dirtied to conform to the other three walls of the storeroom. It had been done so skilfully that apart from the unfinished section the new wall looked just as old as the other three.

On the floor of the storeroom boards had been laid. On these boards were the remaining bricks, pails of water, bags of mortar and sand required to complete the job.

I had hidden some of the contents of my bag on top of the big wardrobe when I was first in my bedroom. Some other things I placed in my pockets before going downstairs.

We had a meal of sorts in the dining-room. Metcalfe cleared the table afterwards and departed to wash up. Howard suggested that we retire to the lounge for more drinks. We did so. Once the lounge door had been closed I decided the time had come to act.

When I held them up with my revolver they were shocked, frightened, angry and puzzled. Puzzled because, although they did not trust me, they could not see what I had to gain by acting in this way. As far as they could see I had to allow Howard to remain master of Ardvreck House to look after the gold hidden in its cellars.

I produced two pairs of handcuffs, threw them on to a couch and told Howard and Adams to put them on. They stood staring at me, still uncertain that there was any sense or ultimate determination in my actions. I told them they had the choice of being shot there and then or of submitting and finding out what I had in mind. My complete sincerity and the reputation I had carefully built up in previous weeks decided them. That, I suppose, and the new look of implacable enmity they read on my face.

They put on the handcuffs. I sat them on a couch with their backs to the door, their hands in their laps while I placed myself opposite them, the gun concealed in my pocket. When Metcalfe knocked at the door – I suppose old habits die hard – I nodded to Howard. He invited Metcalfe in. He was well into the room before I produced the gun. When he was handcuffed I made him pinion his companions' ankles with the lengths of thick window cord I had in my pockets. I treated his ankles in likewise fashion. One by one I released them from the handcuffs only to refasten their hands behind their backs.

I was now in control of the situation. To the three men's threats, questions, entreaties I turned a deaf ear. I ran upstairs, retrieved the coil of rope I had hidden in the bedroom and brought it downstairs. When I re-entered the lounge they were talking furiously among themselves. I replaced their ankle bonds with halters of rope and made them shuffle into the hall. There I ordered them to sit on the treads, their backs to the banister while I roped their handcuffs to it.

That was three days ago.

During the next forty-eight hours I made some immediately necessary preparations. I then waited. I fed and watered my three prisoners, released them in turn to take them to the bathroom before reattaching them to their respective pillars. I also spent some time in the second floor tower room writing the earlier part of this account. Is it my impression that this house has a vile, wretched atmosphere correct or is it my imagination fed by Elaine's account of the things that have been perpetrated here?

When the time had come, I returned to my captives. It was eleven o'clock at night. Standing at the foot of the stairs I addressed them.

'I can now satisfy your curiosity. There is no gold and no diamonds.'

'But the newspaper accounts – ?' Howard, his stubbled face gaunt with fear, yet spoke protestingly as if even now he could not bear to see his dreams of fortune vanish.

'There was a robbery. But I know nothing about it.'

'Then – Then who are you? Why all this? What have we done to you?'

'My name is Peter Cavendish. You know that already. I am the brother of Elaine Milne-Thompson.'

There was silence. I swear a grey sheen of impending death appeared on all three faces simultaneously. I described to them how I had found her, what her final state had been. How she had ended her life.

Adams began to babble pleas for mercy. Howard cursed him to silence. Shivering a little, he could still look me in the eye.

'What are you going to do with us? You could have killed us at any time in the past two days. Why the delay? Why all this charade about getting us to – ?'

He broke off. All colour drained from his face and a look of horror appeared. He had discerned my intentions but dare not speak on the minuscule hope that he was wrong.

But he wasn't.

I released Adams from the banister, led him downstairs. When he saw what faced him he fainted. And so gave no trouble. Metcalfe struggled and I was forced to knock him out. Having dealt with him I went back upstairs for Howard.

I suppose I should have knocked him out and carried him downstairs. But he seemed calm enough – I thought he was anaesthetised with shock – until we reached the cellar storeroom and he faced the unfinished wall. He turned to me.

'For God's sake, Cavendish, have mercy! At least put us out fast!'

'Faster than you put Elaine out, but not as fast as you'd like.'

With that he jerked the upper part of his head forward. He was taller than I and the blow from his head struck me on eye and nose. Dazed, I stumbled over a cement bag and fell. If he had kept his head he might yet have turned the tables. Even with the halter he might have kicked me into unconsciousness. But his only thought was to get away. By the time I had got to my feet again he was in the scullery. I caught up with him as he hurled himself at the kitchen doors in a frenzy. I seized him and dragged him backwards, his screams of terror resounding through the house.

By the time I had dragged him downstairs again into the cellar my resolution was almost gone. But his frenzy suddenly seemed to leave him and without much trouble I got him through the gap in the new wall. I shackled him to the last two pairs of handcuffs I had cemented into the wall forty-eight hours before. His companions, still unconscious, dangled from their own fetters.

And then I bricked them up.

Dawn was breaking by the time I had finished. I slept for twelve hours then continued this account. It is almost finished now. I shall complete it, put it in a small deedbox I brought with me, tie string around it and slip it through the small gap I have left in the wall for that purpose. I shall then cement in the final four bricks. There remains the whitewashing and disguising of the wall, the clearing away of the bags, planks of wood, the –

Arnold Bourne ceased reading, laid the last sheet down thoughtfully.

'The rest of it is on the two scorched sheets. They're so brittle I don't want to try to decipher what's on them in the meantime. Probably need ultra-violet light in any case. However I think we can guess the rest.'

In the Volvo, although the engine was running and the heating was on, it seemed cold. Paul looked at Carol.

'It explains an awful lot,' he said. 'I suppose he packed their clothes, took the family coach and left. I suppose he went back to Africa.' He visualized the three human skeletons hanging from their fetters in the cavity of the ruined house and drew a deep breath. Oh Christ, he thought. Man's inhumanity to man . . .

Carol looked at Meredith.

'The woman Paul saw –'

'What woman?'

Paul repeated his story. Meredith nodded.

'Haven't you realized yet, Mr Wilson, that you are a sensitive?'

'Me!'

'Yes. Think about it. Nothing happened until you and Mrs Wilson arrived. You saw the man in the tower room, you were always around when phenomena occurred. You saw the young woman in the ruins. I think Ardvreck House has brought your latent talent into the open now.'

Carol gazed at Paul.

'I hope you're wrong, Mr Meredith. I really do hope so.' She frowned. 'I'm still trying to understand everything. There seems to have been two types of . . . thing . . . in that house. The weeping, the woman Colin saw, some of the other things that happened. When you think of it, in the light of what you and Paul and Dr Bourne found this morning, all these were almost attempts to draw attention to the cavity and its contents.'

'In what way?'

'Well, the weeping ended in the billiards-room just above the cavity; the woman – Elaine? – led Paul there. Even some of the other things are suggestive. The knotted curtains – bonds? The scattered coal – from the cellars. The rain of whisky and gin – a hint to the wine-cellar?'

Bourne smiled slightly.

'Very ingenious. And the tower of dishes?'

Carol shrugged. Paul remembered his own feelings of claustrophobic confinement in the cellars while they searched them. He felt the sickness return.

'What about the other things?' Joyce asked. 'They were quite different. That thing in your bed.'

Carol shuddered.

'That's what I mean. That thing, and what happened to Sir Henry Fraser's little boy. And Bernard Gray.'

'And the attempt to destroy us all,' Ann interjected.

'Yes. They were something else. What is your opinion on that, Mr Meredith?'

'I don't think I have one beyond a few vague speculations, Mrs Wilson. Howard, Adams and Metcalfe's deaths were violent, mind-crazing and unspeakably horrific. They were buried alive in total darkness. If they didn't suffocate they probably suffered torments of thirst and hunger. They were probably delirious at the end, their minds disintegrating under their agonies. Hate and lust for revenge were certainly ever-present factors. In his account, Peter Cavendish quoted *Othello*. Let me also quote Shakespeare. From *Hamlet*.

> ' "To sleep, perchance to dream. Aye, there's the rub
> For in that sleep of death what dreams may come."

'Remember Dr Wickland and his ideas. Is it conceivably possible that this mysterious world, about which we know so little, allows such nightmares to exist and in certain circumstances affect the living? Who knows?'

Paul twisted round, opened the car door and got out. The air was cool and fresh with the promise of better weather. He walked round the bonnet of the Volvo and stood facing the smoking ruins of Ardvreck House. A faint whirring noise came to his ears. In the pale sky an approaching helicopter caught his attention. Someone on the other side of the sea-loch must have spotted the blaze last night and informed the authorities. Behind him the other doors of the car opened and the others came out. He put his arm about Carol's shoulders and watched the aircraft beat nearer. Like Carol he hoped Meredith was wrong. Wrong about lots of things. But he was not sure that he was.

Lightning Source UK Ltd.
Milton Keynes UK
UKHW040727130819
347891UK00001B/326/P